by
tak
of

6.1l

2·6 A

−5

27

−3 N

15 N

3·0 N

L.26

L.26

THE FLY
IN THE OINTMENT

THE FLY
IN THE OINTMENT

Alice Thomas Ellis

Duckworth

First published in 1989 by
Gerald Duckworth & Co. Ltd.
The Old Piano Factory
43 Gloucester Crescent, London NW1

© 1989 by Alice Thomas Ellis

ISBN 0 7156 2296 X

Photoset in North Wales by
Derek Doyle & Associates, Mold, Clwyd.
Printed in Great Britain by
Billing & Sons Limited, Worcester

FOR COLIN

My coffee had gone cold. It looked, I thought, as though it had died, since it had a grey, inert appearance and only something dead could possibly go cold in such heat. I might have been thinking like this because I was reading the obituary column in an old copy of *The Times* in order to discourage other club members from coming to talk to me, and I was not yet old enough to be cheered by the deaths of strangers. Somebody stood up at a neighbouring table so I read the list of forthcoming marriages with an assumed intense interest, reflecting that strangers who were engaged to each other were even more boring than strangers who had died. Then I saw two names I recognised and immediately I looked up and around to see if there was anyone present who would remember Monica – someone who would appreciate how very peculiar, and indeed amusing, this announcement was. It was quite pointless. Nobody here had met Syl. Nobody here knew the circumstances of our past. Nobody here would be diverted to learn that Syl was going to marry Monica's daughter unless I acquainted them with the facts and I couldn't very well do that. I was already regarded as not *quite*. That was how the women put it: 'Well, darling – Lili is very good

5

company and all that, but she isn't *quite*...' And most of them wouldn't trust their husbands alone with me. Nor could I tell my own husband the details of my last days in England. He was a tolerant man, but there are limits.

I saw him coming towards me across the terrace and stood up waving the newspaper. 'Look,' I said, 'look – Monica's daughter's going to marry Syl.' 'Who?' said Robert. It was an unsatisfactory morning. I poured the dead coffee on to the bank of the Nile and called for a gin.

*

'So,' I said, 'I've decided. I'm coming with you to England.' Clever Robert painted pictures. He was having an exhibition in Soho. I had arranged with God to go regularly to Mass if we could sell a lot of these pictures. Robert said it was too short notice and we couldn't afford it. I said, 'I will sell some jewellery.' Robert said I hadn't got any left. I had. I had some new golden things that my aunt had given me only a short while before. They were an investment. My father, as was the Egyptian custom, had kept all the women of his family, continuing to feel responsible for even the sisters who had married. As a result, whenever my aunts made money – as they frequently did by buying and selling – they thought of it as *family* money and gave me some. They always wanted to invest it for

6

me, to buy a little villa in Portugal, or a share in a little ship, but I would tell them I'd invest it myself in something English and they never felt they could argue with me for my mother had been the *Anglaise* and that made me a little different, not *quite* like them. And then I would spend it, confident that my astute relations would make and give me some more. I seldom had to ask, and never twice. Robert wasn't rich so the extra money was necessary. I said, 'My aunt gave me a *parterre...*' Robert interrupted to remind me, briefly, that he wished I wouldn't take money from my aunts. I said, it wasn't money, it was gold things, but we both knew they were things to sell. Robert could not rid himself of the idea that accepting money from *anybody* was 'sponging'. I could see his point, for I had been a pupil at the English school in Alexandria and there I had learned that many English people felt this way. Monica had felt that way even when she was a little girl. Nevertheless I couldn't really understand it, for was not family *family?* And was not the good of the family the good of all its members? Robert often made me feel alien – oriental and exotic. In the *salons* of my aunts I became languid and pale like a lily and with Robert I could feel my skin grow darker, my body smaller and my eyes glowing. I went barefoot. I suppose that was why I had married him.

I said, 'It is years since I felt the chill of an English winter, oh my dearest. I want to walk in the fog and kick up the dead leaves.' 'Why?' asked Robert, in a reasonable tone, and I saw that I had

7

approached the matter from the wrong angle.
'Monica is my oldest friend,' I said. 'I have known
her all my life and I have known Margaret since she
was a tiny little girl. I must go to her wedding.
When she was a tiny little child I gave my *word* that
I would go to her wedding.' 'You haven't been
asked yet,' said Robert.

*

Oh, the horrible journey and the horrible cold! I
had had a little fever before I left home and, as
always, had imagined that, by contrast, it would be
wonderful to be chilled to the bone. Now I could
think of nothing more delightful than sitting in an
African garden, baking like a cake. I could feel the
fog going up my nose and there was nothing I
could do about it. If I complained to Robert I
should simply look a fool, for I had brought it all
on myself. I was going to have to make the best of
it.

We were staying at a dreadful little hotel on the
Uxbridge Road. It seemed to me extravagantly,
unnecessarily dreadful so I wasted no time in
writing to Monica with congratulations on her
daughter's engagement. I could have telephoned
but letters are safer: more formal, and demanding
of a response from the well brought up English
gentlewoman. She wrote back immediately inviting
us to stay with her, and I danced a bit on the

disgusting linoleum of the dreadful hotel bedroom. Robert had gone to the gallery where his pictures were to be shown, so I had some time to decide how to break the news to him. I have found that men often do not like staying in other people's houses. I don't know why. Besides he was bound to assume I had been 'sponging' again.

When I heard his footsteps outside the bedroom door I lit another cigarette. I had already smoked a packet and I had put a lot of shillings into the meter, so the gas-fire had been hissing all afternoon. 'God,' said Robert, 'what a fug!'

'It doesn't matter, my darling,' I said. 'We're not staying.' Robert put his hat on the bed. He was being difficult, but that didn't matter either. I always got my own way. I told him there were cockroaches behind the skirting board, and the lorries roaring down the Uxbridge Road had kept me awake all night. I said the proprietor of this hotel had not changed the sheets since the previous occupant, but had merely ironed them *in situ* on the bed. I said I was convinced the previous occupant had been diseased, for I had found shreds of bloodstained tissue sticking to the sides of the wastepaper-basket. I did all the talking while Robert took his coat and his shoes off. I had hoped that he would say we couldn't afford to go anywhere better so that I could announce that we were going to save money by staying with Monica, but he said, 'I suppose you've got hold of Monica,' and I remembered that he knew me well. Sometimes I thought that he didn't like me much.

'It makes perfect sense,' I said. 'Besides Monica leads a most dull life and we will add some interest and glamour to it. This is a kindness we are doing.' It was *true*.

I left the dreadful hotel that afternoon. Robert had gone back into the city in order, I think, to assert his independence. The proprietor of the dreadful hotel took our suitcases down to the cab and stood watching as it drove away. I waved to him and sat back feeling a sense of comfort and gratification since I had done *nothing* to charm him and he was still sorry to see me go. There I was, going to a better place, and there was this unattractive stranger mourning my departure from his dreadful hotel. Clever Lili. I had some tiny misgivings about Robert, but I knew he'd come round in the end. Apart from the fact that he loved me he was much too sensible to turn down the offer of free hospitality. There was a remote chance that he might stay with some other friend, but most of the people we knew in London lived in discomfort in little flats or single rooms or studios, sharing bathrooms and washing their paint-brushes in the lavatory. They thought it was bohemian. Robert was really no fonder of squalor than I was myself. He'd be along in the course of time. Anyway all his clothes and his toothbrush were in a suitcase next to the driver.

*

Croydon was much as I remembered it. I was not your usual sort of foreigner; not convinced that only Park Lane was fit for human habitation. I liked Croydon, and I found Monica's house very comfortable. It might have been in the country with its big garden and its big rooms. If I could have taken it to Râs-et-Tin I could have lived in it happily for the rest of my life. As it was, I enjoyed its Englishness. Robert didn't like it. He said it was an architectural abortion, but I really didn't care what it looked like from outside. My own little villa – which was all I had left now – didn't look very good from outside. Inside it was different: half oriental, half *rive gauche*. Very *me*. I was a cosmopolitan and happy anywhere if it was warm. I had gypsy blood, for I was an Egyptian. Do you see?

'Oh, Monica,' I said, 'my dearest, how lovely to see you after all this time.' I kissed her on both cheeks, behaving in a foreign way, because it would be more interesting for her and the little Margaret. The little Margaret I didn't recognise for I hadn't seen her for years and years since she was a child. I just assumed it was her because it couldn't really have been anybody else and I said I must congratulate her on her forthcoming nuptials, and Monica said one was meant to congratulate the groom, not the bride, so I said I trusted she was doing the right thing and Monica said one was supposed to wish the bride *happiness*. So I did that and I talked rather a lot because it is always a little awkward meeting again people you have not seen

11

for a long time, and I was remembering the things that Marie Claire had told me that I knew I was not supposed to know, and really it came as a relief when Monica asked where Robert was.

I said vaguely with some large and meaningless gestures that he'd had to go to the gallery. Monica would make allowances for us because I was not wholly English and Robert was an artist. I said he would be along in the course of time and asked if I might go to my room. Margaret took one of the suitcases and I noticed that she did not look healthy. She didn't look as though she would be able to lift a matchbox let alone a suitcase, and also she looked half-witted. When we got to the bedroom she put down the suitcase and stood in the middle of the floor with her shoulders hunched. I thought how satisfying it would be to shake people who stood looking like that. To take them and shake them until their eyelids rolled up in astonishment and they were made to understand that there was life on other planets and other life on this planet. Margaret was locked in some solitary misery and unaware even of *me*. I couldn't have that. I never, never did like to be seen as negligible, not so much out of vanity as because it made *me* doubt my own existence. I was a dancer and I danced because people *have* to look at people dancing. They can't be ignored. No, I wasn't that bad. I felt sorry for Margaret. I really did. I was not going to question her about the events in Egypt when Monica had sent her off to stay with Marie Claire, although I was curious to have her version.

12

Marie Claire – who, I will say immediately, was a terrible pain in the neck – had said that poor little Margaret had fallen madly in love with her son, the silly little Nour. Marie Claire suffered under the delusion that both she and her child were utterly irresistible to persons of the opposite sex, and while it was not impossible that Margaret had indeed fallen prey to the wretched boy, I had laughed dismissively and told Marie Claire not to derange herself about it. That had annoyed her. I told her I had spoken to Margaret's friends, the nuns at the convent where I went to Mass when I stayed with Marie Claire and they had said she was merely homesick. I was lying. Mother Joseph had said she believed that the *petite anglaise* had a true vocation, but I wasn't going to tell Marie Claire that because she would instantly say that broken-hearted girls often took the veil. I hadn't really been very interested in Margaret and her problems for, after all, I hadn't seen her for years, and Marie Claire had grown angry. She said Nour had told her that Margaret had done something *wicked* and I asked what. She wouldn't tell me and, without actually saying so, I had indicated with smiles and flourishes that I knew Nour to be a terrible, *terrible* liar.

I said to Margaret, 'You look as though you haven't been sleeping.' She jumped and muttered something. I lit a cigarette and began to think about the awful boringness of unpacking the suitcases which, after all, I'd only packed an hour or so before in the dreadful hotel. I was not looking my best; not exactly *travel-stained* because what was there to stain you these days? Boats and trains and taxis kept you out of the mud; we had encountered no blood and no one had thrown wine over me. I was unstained, but my clothes were crumpled. I looked at Margaret, wondering whether I could say to her, 'Darling, would you be a little heavenly angel and just press this blouse for me?' But it wouldn't have been any use. You can't really ask people to do things for you if you can't see any signs of life in them. There isn't any point.

*

'And how is Syl?' I asked when we had sat down to dinner. I asked partly out of politeness, because why should I care how he was after all this time, and partly out of curiosity because I couldn't imagine why she was going to marry him. He was twice her age. 'Is he still handsome?' I said, because it was the politest thing I could think of to say, and Monica said he flew around playing squash and golf and kept himself very fit. Margaret said nothing to add to this unappealing picture and I began to feel rather old, for Syl and I were the same age, were we not, and what was all this talk about keeping in trim? I *was* in trim. I didn't need to play stupid games or jump up and down all over the place. I was fit as a flea. Healthy Lili. Oh, naughty, nasty Margaret to make me feel suddenly old.

14

Monica said, 'Tell Lili what you thought of Egypt,' as though the girl was a parrot to utter a phrase and be given a nut. 'It-was-very-nice,' said Margaret in her little dull voice as though she feared I would be offended if she said she'd hated it. I don't *own* Egypt – I thought – I'm not *Cleopatra* – I don't care if you hated the sight of the Valley of the Kings and all the *accoutrements* of Tutankhamun. I don't care if you detested the *fellahin* and *feluccas* and *falafel*. Nothing to do with me.

'What did you think of Marie Claire?' I asked her, and I wondered whether perhaps she *had* been in love with the beastly little Nour and was marrying old Syl on the rebound.

'She-was-very-kind,' came the response. I might have known.

'She's very clever,' said Monica.

I wasn't having that. '*Kind* I will allow,' I said, 'Marie Claire is not ungenerous...' (I thought this magnanimous of me) '...but she hasn't got the sense of a chicken.'

'Oh Lili,' said Monica. 'She was cleverer than all of us in school. She was top of the class, time after time.'

This was *really* annoying. Marie Claire had always cheated. She'd have *aides memoires* painted in henna on her arms under her long sleeves and on her legs up to where her socks stopped. I had sometimes cheated too when I could be bothered, but I had never cared about exam results in the way the others did. Monica didn't cheat. She *swotted*. She'd been a stupid girl in many ways. I said, 'What I said

15

was – she didn't have any *sense*.' Monica looked at me as though she found me ridiculous. Any minute now I should find myself squabbling as I'd squabbled at school and I lit a cigarette and breathed deeply. I must not allow myself to be drawn into an undignified wrangle. Dinner had been more or less all right, the beds were soft and the rooms warm. I must behave like a grateful and courteous guest, not an undisciplined schoolgirl – no matter how maddening Monica could be, and I was beginning to remember just *how* maddening that was.

'You always did talk frightful nonsense,' she said to me in a tone half reproving, half indulgent. I was speechless.

Suddenly Margaret spoke. 'She was *daft*,' she said, and in the twinkling of an eye I saw the child in a different light. Not only did it appear that she held convictions of her own – she held the correct convictions. I reminded myself again how unwise it was to leap to conclusions before a proper period of observation, and I regarded her closely for the first time with these new eyes.

'How you can say that', said Monica to her daughter, 'when Marie Claire was so good to you, I really can't imagine.' She spoke of the ingratitude of guests and I was glad I'd held my tongue earlier. She was really cross. She was cross with me; but just as the good guest cannot roar at her hostess, no more can the good hostess roar at the guest, so she was taking it out on Margaret. Now that I was looking at Margaret properly I saw that she was not

16

as ordinary as I had thought. Not quite. She didn't answer her mother, not – I thought – because she was afraid to, but because she knew it would be a waste of time and energy. She had bones and features and she sat still.

*

She didn't look to me like a girl who was about to get married. Or maybe she did? It all depended on expectation. There were girls – they were usually the ones who had been good at games – who sort of leapt at marriage with their hair flying and a glint of lasciviousness in their eye. They flew greedily around, buying things to put in their new houses, and hats to put on their heads, and shoes and frocks and knickers and nighties. They were grabbers. They would grab their husband on the wedding night and never willingly relinquish him. They would if they were the *first* to find someone better, but if they were enjoying him and suddenly caught him straying they would cut up his clothes and follow him to his places of assignation where they would stamp and scream curses, and throw things. If they were driving a car they would try and run him over. I had known several such – the kind who made their own marriages. Then there were the kind whose marriages were arranged for them. Many of my friends fell into this category, but they were not usually Christian and most of them had hated games. They went placidly along with the arrangements and let themselves be wed. Sometimes they lived lives of contentment, and if they didn't it was just too bad. Margaret looked like someone being led to the wedding. 'Is everything planned for the day?' I asked. 'Who's coming? Is Derek coming?' Derek was Monica's ex.

'Yes', said Monica, 'Derek's coming. And his family. Jennifer and Christopher are going to be page and bridesmaid.' She sounded smug and I looked at her closely. Monica was one of the grabbers. She had written to me when Derek married again – not when he left her but when he married again. She had expressed herself in unguarded terms and I daresay when she'd posted the letter she'd wished she hadn't. Something must have happened to reconcile her to the situation. On a moment's reflection it was pretty clear what it was: nothing dramatic like a conversion, a change of heart, a surge of generous forgiveness. No. Looking round at the creamy comfort which characterised Monica's mode of life I realised that she'd grabbed *everything*. Derek was a dreary type of man even by Monica's standards and she'd probably been only too glad to be rid of him, once she'd understood that she could grab and grab and leave him and his new wife to struggle along as best they could, living on alms if need be. She'd kept everything – the knives and forks we were eating with, the tablecloth under the dinner service which could only have been a wedding present, not being the sort of thing you'd buy for yourself. She'd grabbed all the wedding presents and everything that they'd since acquired. I rather admired her. Another thought occurred to me: 'What's she like?' I asked. 'What's the new wife like?'

'A nice little thing,' said Monica.

'Aha,' I said, for these words conveyed much meaning. They meant colourless, dowdy, poor and tedious. I could *see* her, this new wife. She made her own clothes and her wardrobe smelled of moth balls. Her feet smelled of feet for she could not afford much hot water to wash. I would not be one ounce surprised if her feet were flat. Her shoulders would smell of tears and the vomit of children.

'Her name is *Cynthia*,' said Monica. All my suppositions were correct, for what could a *Cynthia* be but tiresome? 'Oh, yuk,' I said, and for a moment Monica and I were in accord.

*

I got up early. To be truthful I hadn't slept very well. To be absolutely truthful I was a tiny bit worried. I brushed my hair and it went crackle, crackle. I wasn't very pleased with my hair – it wouldn't shine because I had had a fever. It was going a bit grey when I looked at it closely. See how truthful I am being. Truthfully, I had forgotten what colour it really was. My aunts had hennaed it since I was a tiny little baby. It was due for a fresh application. Oh how troublesome everything could

19

be. The curls were natural – oh, all right, I gave them a little help with the curling tongs when it was necessary, but basically they were real. Now the treacherous hair would not behave. I should have to wear a hat.

Where was Robert? Where was Robert? *Where was Robert?*

Of course he would telephone soon. He would telephone or just arrive at the house. He always did. No cause to worry. Nobody ever left Lili. Not for long. Well, almost nobody. I was certainly growing older, for there comes a time in life when you must face the truth. There are two times – once when you are very young and think in terms of absolutes; and then when you have spent your years lying a bit and scheming a little because you must survive, then the time comes again, when you no longer think in terms of absolutes. It had come. I didn't really know why. Perhaps because once you no longer feel invincible the truth is all you have left...

I said to the woman – Oh, oh, whatever happened to the girl? Where had that girl gone? – I said to the woman in the looking-glass: 'Pull yourself together, Lili.' I spoke firmly. Peering closely I put lipstick on that woman's lips, mascara on her eyelashes, powder on her nose. And there she was. The girl was back. I dressed her in a very simple frock of black jersey. A very simple Paris frock; and I pulled in my stomach, for the girl had had no stomach at all, and I didn't want to let her down.

'All dressed up and nowhere to go, eh?' said Monica as I came into the kitchen. An irritating remark, you must agree. 'Where's Robert?' she asked, as I ignored this conversational gambit.

'He is terribly taken up with his exhibition, Monica,' I said, in the serious tones I use when speaking of work or money.

'All night?' asked Monica.

'Very possibly,' I said. 'He has to spend much time with the gallery owner. They were quite probably up all night.' Monica knew nothing of the world of art so she couldn't argue. It was maddening for her.

'What do you want for breakfast?' she enquired, sounding rather grudging. I thought I might take the opportunity to have a real English breakfast – bacon and eggs – but I wouldn't have been able to eat it. Not all of it, and Monica would be cross with me.

'I will have just a *croissant* and some coffee,' I said.

'We don't have *croissants* in Croydon,' said Monica, and by now she sounded rather grim. 'And until I get round to putting in an order at Selfridges we don't have any coffee beans. Will Nescafé do?'

Oh. I should have to be careful. Monica was under strain. Probably she found Margaret recalcitrant. I must be good. Two difficult females under her roof would be more than she could endure. Stupid people, contrary to popular belief, are not good at endurance like dumb animals.

They crack and behave unfairly, blaming the innocent for things they haven't done. I said, like a sweet and grateful innocent, that I would love a cup of Nescafé and a weeny-teeny bit of toast. With perhaps a little marmalade. She was already making toast, so that was all right.

'I'm taking Margaret her breakfast in bed,' she announced, rather, I thought, as a person might remark that she was going to find a leper and give him a smacking kiss. A martyr in search of martyrdom. I would have offered to take up the tray myself, but my coffee would have gone cold, and we all know how much I hate cold coffee. Can't abide it.

'It's easier in the end,' she said, slapping toast on a plate. 'Better than having the kitchen full of people first thing in the morning with the day ahead.'

There were many responses I could have made to this. I could have asked why we did not break our fast in the dining-room. I could have asked why it mattered, having the kitchen full of people. I could have pointed out that every morning the day lay ahead, and there was really no reason to mention it, for I needed no reminder. But would that have been wise? No, it would not. So I ate my toast very carefully and brushed up the crumbs with my finger. The telephone rang and I forgot about the crumbs and flew to answer it. It would be Robert calling, for it had to be Robert. I willed it to be Robert and it was. So that was all right.

'Did I hear the phone,' asked Monica, when she

came down. I was in trouble again – answering *her* telephone.

'I answered it,' I said, 'to save you the trouble of flying downstairs and breaking your head on the parquet.'

'Who was it?' she enquired, not really mollified by my care.

'It was Robert,' I said. 'Soon he will be coming.' Oddly enough this seemed to cheer Monica. Perhaps she missed having a man around. There were women, I knew, who felt that life was incomplete without a man around. No reason to cook. No reason, really, to comb your hair. Perhaps, underneath, Monica felt like that. I did myself. Sometimes I did and to be honest sometimes I didn't. It was a matter of mood. Sometimes, when I was little, it was better when my father was away and I was alone with my aunts and my mother. It was easier to laugh and there seemed more to laugh at, but then when he came he brought presents and a certain sense of excitement. He brought me a monkey once. I wonder what happened to it.

Down came Margaret – rather like rain – grey and not cheerful. I said, 'Here comes the bride', and I thought – poor girl. How ridiculous. People who look like that don't get *married*. They sit in corners and people pretend not to notice them. I said out of curiosity: 'When will we be seeing Syl again?' I wasn't all that curious about this, actually. I wanted to see her reaction to his name. She didn't react at all, just said he'd be round in the evening, and nothing more.

23

She made no effort at all and I began to feel depressed. It was cold outside and I could see things blowing about. I said: 'We can have a party.' Monica would probably quite enjoy a small party, I thought. Then, on the other hand, if she caught me planning parties in her parlour without asking her she'd be mad with me again. 'Maybe we won't have a party,' I said. Quite often I didn't like parties; nasty, noisy occasions. Can't hear yourself think. Too hot. Squashed. When I was Margaret's age I didn't like parties at all unless I was asked to dance. I don't mean May-I-have-the-next-waltz type of thing – I mean me dancing all by myself in a clear space so that everyone could see me. Graceful Lili. Such *talent*.

Monica came in worrying about dinner and looking quite, quite as depressing as the weather. The weather, by contrast, began to look almost inviting. A brisk walk would be good for me. Monica hadn't got enough chops for dinner, poor soul, not if extra people were coming, so I said I'd go and get her some.

'Come on, Margaret,' I said. 'We shall wrap ourselves up warmly and go and buy these chops.' It was nice of me to take Margaret too because she was not easy to converse with. On the other hand she, I imagined, would know the way to the butcher's shop and I didn't want to go wandering all over Croydon in the wind hunting for meat. No fun really. Ach, it was cold out there. I said so. I promised myself that I would buy a new coat. A big, warm English coat for the English winds.

24

English people, I remembered, often went for walks just for the sake of it. Not to go anywhere or do anything – just walk. Silly, I call it. It was very monotonous putting one foot in front of the other.

Margaret, who until then had not opened her mouth, told me that she used to walk in Egypt. Just that. 'I used to walk in Egypt,' she said. How interesting. A lot of people walk in Egypt. *Thousands* of them, up and down the *gisr* and all around the towns.

'How did Syl propose?' I asked. This was something I actually wanted to know – for all sorts of reasons. Well, I was curious for a variety of reasons.

Margaret appeared to give this some thought. I was changing my mind about her again. She was worse than ordinary. Was she, perhaps, mentally retarded? 'He asked me to marry him so I said I would,' she finally told me. Well, what an earth-shattering revelation. Fancy that. How truly amazing. 'Why?' I asked.

'I don't know,' she said, and she looked very sad, so sad that now I began to feel sorry for her. It was no use my pretending that I thought this marriage was a good idea because it wasn't. It was a silly idea. Remember – I knew Syl. I said, 'I wonder if he's queer?' and then thought that perhaps I should not have. It wasn't very tactful, was it? Too late now, anyway. I had sometimes wondered that in the past. 'I mean he's getting on', I said, 'and living with his mother and never got married yet and all that.'

'He's had girlfriends,' said Margaret, as one who

states a fact. *I* knew *that*. I wondered if she knew how many. There'd been a time when he changed girls as often as he changed socks. It had looked like a kind of insanity, and sometimes I'd wondered if he wished he'd been a girl, surrounding himself as he did with such heaps of the creatures. Everybody lost count. The minute one affair was over – and often before – he'd be in love again and always with somebody *unlikely*, somebody who, you felt, would have remained forever on the shelf if Syl hadn't reached up and brought her down and dusted her. He seemed to have an ability to see something in the dullest, plainest female; some spark imperceptible to the rest of the world. Having perceived this twinkle he would set about fanning it in his mind to a positive pyre, a great glorious leaping thing of flame and heat. He would describe the new girl in these fire-lit terms and bring her to meet you, and when he did you'd find the sort of girl you bought your stockings from, or who dealt out your prescription over the chemist's counter. Yes, all right. I *am* a snob. I am particularly a snob in matters of sex. Monica too used to be disgusted. Why did she permit her daughter now to be engaged to him? I thought it was very bad of Monica. I didn't understand her. It was all too peculiar. Maybe I had been away too long and forgotten how the English behaved. What an annoying thought. I am particularly fond of understanding.

The butcher's shop was bright and orderly. It gave a rather comfortable impression which was remarkable considering its purpose. Nice clean bits of animals hung around in neat rows. It was warmer in there out of the wind and I was quite sorry to leave. There were all manner of cuts of meat I hadn't seen for years and the butcher bragged about them. He was as proud of his liver as if it had been his own. I was a bit worried about mine for I drank too much. Oh yes I did. I knew it and I sincerely meant to mend my ways. If Monica intended to stuff us with meat at every meal then I should have to persuade her to give us extra vegetables too. We didn't eat much meat at home. It wasn't really very good. I would have to buy garlic myself since Monica would be bound to consider it vulgar and it was essential for health, cleansing the blood and clearing the skin. I like to look after myself even if I do drink too much. *Because* I drink too much.

*

Robert was in a rage. He claimed several reasons for this rage – good and sufficient reasons, he said – Croydon, and gallery owners and such things – and me. 'Oh nonsense, Robert,' I said. 'It will all be all right on the night.' Monica had put on some scent. 'Be nice to Monica,' I said in his ear, and I pulled it because I was glad he was there, after all. He gave me what I can only describe as a cold look, which I ignored, but he did set about being nice to

Monica. He sat down beside her and conversed –
mostly about past events, for that was all they had
in common, apart from their humanity, which
didn't offer much in the way of social chitchat. I
was, I confess, relieved that Robert was there. He
wouldn't have left me for ever, wouldn't have left
me for long, but when they're not there you can
never be absolutely certain – either as to where they
are or whether they truly will be coming back. Not
absolutely certain; not unless they have huge
possessions and a special chair and slippers that
they mind about. Our life wasn't like that. Even the
house at home was more mine than Robert's. All
that held Robert to me was me, and while that
should have been sufficient (and indeed was really)
sometimes when my hair wouldn't shine and I
looked in the looking-glass in the cold grey light –
well, sometimes I wondered just a little. Just a *very*
little.

I was so glad to see Robert making his effort and
being nice to Monica that I'd hardly taken any
notice of Syl. He hadn't changed. He was just the
same. Same clothes, same face, same Syl. 'How well
you look,' I said. I meant well-preserved, for that
was the impression he gave. He had put his arm
about Margaret's shoulders and she moved away
towards me saying, 'What were you like when you
were young?' What a question out of nowhere!
Why did she ask it? Did I look a hag? Was I perhaps
decaying under her eyes? Monica heard too and
seemed to take it personally. 'Do grow up,' she said
to her child, which was ironic when you think about

it, since she was offended at the suggestion she was
no longer young and the more Margaret grew the
older *she'd* be. But then Monica was never what you
could call logically-minded.

'I take care of myself,' said Syl. 'I like to keep fit.'

This conjured a melancholy picture of Syl
jumping up and down, beating his arms around
and pouring with sweat.

'Press-ups?' I asked gloomily and felt his biceps.
'Mmm,' I said.

'You look well too,' he remarked without
conviction. Syl and I had got off on the wrong foot
with all this talk of health and youth. There was an
anti-social air of competitiveness, regret and envy
floating about. You'd never have thought – well,
never mind!'

Dinner seemed endless with those ghastly old
chops. Monica had graciously permitted me to
make the soup and that was all right. I'd used up
the spinach she'd been going to serve with the
chops and put a lot of garlic in it too. I liked doing a
little bit of cooking when I didn't really need to, but
Monica had hung around making critical queries –
'Do you have to use *so* much garlic? Why are you
taking all the ribs out of the spinach?' – and I
decided I wouldn't help in the kitchen any more.
We could always eat out quite a lot, Robert and I. It
took him ages to cope with his chop and his gravy
and potatoes. I felt quite impatient, for it was the
sort of food he'd been brought up on. He should
have learned how to eat it by now. Margaret drank
too much and didn't say anything. Nor did Monica,

29

and I think Syl was sulking, so Robert and I did our world-famous double-act, performed before all the crowned Heads of Europe and the East. Sometimes I thought that together we might be the reincarnation of Abû Nowwâs. Robert told anecdotes and I added to them. We'd dined out that way more times than I could count. I was beginning to get fed up with it so I was glad when Margaret went to bed. Robert went to bed too and Syl went home and I was left to help Monica clear the table. I didn't offer to help wash up. What if I broke one of her wedding present plates? It is very difficult being a guest. The best thing is to be amusing and keep out of the way.

I offered an added bonus and suggested she leave the washing-up till the morning. 'Come and sit down,' I said, 'and tell me all about *everything*.'

'I'm a bit tired,' said Monica, sitting in an armchair and sagging. 'This wedding...'

'You're obviously doing too much,' I said in a solicitous voice. 'Poor darling, it doesn't seem fair.' I don't know what I meant by that, but it went down well.

'Oh Lili, you've no idea,' she said. 'Bringing up a child on your own is no joke.'

'No, it can't be,' I said. Why should it be? No, I didn't say that. I just thought it.

I said rather warily: 'Margaret seems a good girl though.' I wished to compliment Monica's skill in raising this good girl without making light of her achievement in doing it all by herself. 'She's a credit to you,' I added, inspired. 'A really nice girl.' This was praise enough for Monica to allow herself to express some misgivings.

'She's so quiet,' she said. 'She seems to have no go in her at all. I thought when I sent her off to stay with Marie Claire it would do her good – make her see something of the world, make her come out of herself. You know...'

'A lot of people would be glad to have a daughter like Margaret,' I said. Oops – wrong thing to say. I was getting tired.

'They wouldn't if they had to live with her,' said Monica sharply 'You've no idea what a strain it is. She just moons about like a dying duck and she makes no attempt to do anything for herself. I have to think of everything.'

She sounded over-wrought. Any minute now she'd lose her temper or burst into tears. I said: 'You're worried aren't you?' By this time, you see, I felt sorry for her. I really did.

'Oh yes,' she said, wearily. 'I'm worried. I'll be glad when the wedding's over, only...'

'What?' I asked.

Monica stirred in her chair. 'I don't know if she's ready. I don't know... I've never discussed anything with her. I haven't...'

Enlightenment broke upon me. Of course Margaret would have told her mother nothing of the ratty little Nour. 'You don't think she's a virgin, do you?' I cried, wishing simultaneously that I had not, for the events in Egypt, from what little I had gathered, must remain forever shrouded in secrecy or else there would be the most unholy *brouhaha*

31

and I would get the blame for being indiscreet.

Happily Monica's stupidity came to my aid. She gasped like a goldfish. 'Lili, you don't think Syl...'

I said in my relief, 'Darling, you can be so stupid sometimes...' There was a sound from the kitchen and we both listened. 'It was nothing,' I said. 'There's nobody there. No, I just meant – is she a virgin? I didn't mean she wasn't. I don't think Syl would sully his bride, do you?'

Monica looked doubtful. 'Oh look here, Monica,' I said, 'we all know what Syl was like, but that was years ago. He must have grown up a bit since then.' I was not being frank. I saw no reason to suppose that Syl had changed at all. Why should he have? I hadn't. If he hadn't slept with Margaret I bet it wasn't his fault. On the other hand it was just possible... 'If he is truly in love,' I said with my tongue in my cheek, 'he will respect Margaret, will he not?'

'I suppose so,' said Monica, and from her tone I gathered that that was not really what was worrying her. It was something else. 'I sometimes wonder,' said Monica, 'whether she'll *ever* grow up.'

*

Robert was rather alarmingly quiet. He had been since he arrived. Quiet and polite. I didn't like the signs. He was seldom openly angry with me, for when he was I got angry too and that was

32

dangerous. I don't mean I'd have killed him, but when two people lose their tempers one of them always says more than she intends because one of them – at least – feels she must win at all costs, and I have a reckless streak. It is an important part of my character and I cannot erase it, but I like to keep it under control. Robert called it 'showing off' because he'd been taught in school to despise spontaneity. He was hitting the top of a boiled egg with an egg spoon in a concentrated, silent sort of fashion. It made me nervous.

'The thing about marriage,' I said, too loudly, for being made nervous also made me bad-tempered, 'is that it must be exclusive.' Don't ask me why I said that. I wasn't thinking about the wedding. I wasn't thinking about anything much. It just popped out. Nobody else was saying anything after all, so it was good of me to bring a little cultured conversation to this breakfast table. I'm not being truthful, I said it to please Robert. Robert didn't look pleased. He didn't look anything except like a man eating a boiled egg on a winter's morning, while Monica looked contemptuous. I don't think she meant to look like that for she hadn't got enough brains to *be* contemptuous. It was only her expression but it was irritating. I went on. 'We learn nothing from promiscuity,' I said, 'just that there's very little to choose between one man and another.' I often talk like that when I'm drunk, but seldom first thing in the morning. I was more shaken than I'd realised. Robert had disappeared behind *The Times*. Oh, damn. Might as well be hanged for a sheep as a

33

lamb. I was getting everything wrong. 'In order to understand ourselves,' I said, making one of those honest attempts to clarify matters which led you further into the mud, 'we need to understand each other, and to do that we must live together for a long time. Exclusively.' Even I could see that this didn't mean anything. I knew what I meant but I couldn't seem to express it. I meant it was better to understand one thing properly, using one example (well, all right – one man, one husband) rather than go flying round exploring the possibilities of hundreds of them. I *believed* that. Robert lowered *The Times* and looked at me. Monica spoke: 'What have *you* learned, Lili?' she asked.

Great heavens – she *was* being contemptuous.

I floundered. I felt like a person dancing on a river bank when, lo, the bit she's dancing on breaks away and there she is hopping about like a lunatic on a lump of sinking turf. The way of the entertainer is fraught with danger – with mis-understandings and the risk of failure. And now Robert was looking at me. I began to get really cross. I lost the thread of my argument. Anyway, what did I care? 'Oh, I don't know,' I said. 'Isn't it obvious? All you learn from sleeping around is that men are much the same.'

Robert spoke: 'So are women,' he said.

I was furious. I know it was my own fault for talking philosophically over breakfast; for saying the sort of things that are normally only said in smoke-filled rooms after dark, after dinner, after several bottles of something or other. Nevertheless

34

he had no right to say what he said; to humiliate me before Monica.

'I'm not like other women,' I said. 'I'm different.' Perhaps it was the cold and the greyness that were making me unsubtle – making me vulnerable. Making me sound ordinary and – yes – making me sound like other women.

'Yes,' said Robert, 'you *are* different.' His tone was sardonic. I changed the subject. 'What are you thinking about, Margaret?' I enquired. I might have saved my breath, for she replied that she was thinking about what I'd been saying. 'Don't listen to me,' I said. 'I talk a lot of nonsense.' It was sufficiently irritating to have been forced into making such a statement without what happened next. Monica repeated my words. 'Don't fill her head with nonsense,' she said. 'Only a fool would marry for love. Anyone with any sense uses her head when it comes to marriage – chooses someone with a bit of character; someone with good solid qualities.'

I think she was referring to Syl and this was enough to make me blink, apart from the fact that what she said had absolutely nothing to do with what I'd been saying.

'People don't sleep with people because of their good solid qualities,' I said, also with seeming irrelevance. (Monica doubtless thought of herself as having good solid qualities and no one was sleeping with her.) I was glad to see that this had annoyed her. She said nothing. I thought it was high time I dropped the discussion before I really

35

put my foot in it. 'We're off to town,' I said. 'I'm taking Margaret, too.' At the moment I didn't want to be alone with Robert. He was clearly still displeased with me. Quite unjustifiably, in my view, but there you are. Men take offence at the slightest thing.

'I don't really want to go out,' said Margaret.

'Oh yes you do,' said her mother. 'It'll do you good.' She was leaping at the chance of a day's respite from her daughter. She looked determined.

'What'll you wear?' I asked Margaret hastily before she could argue.

'She can wear her grey tweed,' said Monica, beginning to gather up the breakfast plates.

'I'll go and look in her wardrobe,' I said. 'I like looking in other people's wardrobes.' It was true. I sometimes had a dream that I'd been given a house and I went through all the rooms, along the verandahs, looking in other people's wardrobes and chests of drawers. The trouble with this dream was that in the centre of the house lay a vast palm-shaded courtyard and I was never permitted in there. Not ever. It belonged to somebody else. Poor Lili. Oh well.

Margaret's clothes were what you'd expect, but I lent her a jumper of my own and some scent. With a dash of make-up she didn't look too dull. She had a kind of distinction – almost. If she'd concentrated she could have looked rather beautiful, but I was in a hurry and had no time just then to start on artistic endeavours. I could have made her look quite different – but then, what was the point? I'd have

36

got no thanks for it. Besides, why should I create a beauty? I was the beauty here. Who needs two? I was ashamed of this thought. Selfish; unworthy of me. I made Monica lend Margaret her pearls and gave a little lecture on the power of dress.

'Since you're so keen on clothes, Lili,' said Monica, 'you can help me alter her wedding dress.'

'OK,' I said. Real, tangible help from me would do much to reconcile Monica to our presence.

Robert's brother had let us have his car. He was away so he didn't need it. He hadn't wanted us to have it, but he couldn't think of a good reason for refusing. I said, 'I hope we get a good lunch.' I was feeling a bit undernourished.

'Don't expect too much,' said Robert. 'He's in an economical frame of mind.'

'We speak of Robert's gallery owner,' I explained to Margaret. She said, 'Won't he mind if I come too?'

'Who cares?' said Robert. We were both mad with the wretched man who conspicuously failed to appreciate us. He should never have been concerned with art when all he really minded about was money. He hadn't even offered to put us up.

'Is it difficult selling paintings?' asked Margaret.

I felt we must have been careless if she was so aware of the undertones to what we were saying. 'Not at all,' I said. 'Not if they're perfectly superb and they've got me to help sell them. You must watch me at the opening....'

Robert kept interrupting me and I had to make an effort to remain cheerful and positive.

37

I spoke for some minutes on the benefits of being married to a creative person – the added interest and challenge, the absence of boredom. I believe Robert found me unconvincing. He said: 'I told you not to give up dancing.' He spoke too gently for my liking.

I said that I was sick of dancing. I told the truth – the pure, plain truth – which was that I was tired of dancing, and I'd rather spend the time with Robert. Of course it didn't sound like the truth. It sounded as though I was generously pretending that I didn't care about abandoning my own career in order to further Robert's. And it wasn't the whole truth – which was that I was desperately sick of dancing, at that time, lonely and frightened and aching in every limb. You wouldn't believe some of the places I'd danced in. My aunts never knew. Nobody really knew, except perhaps Robert... I said, 'I didn't want to go dancing round the world. Do you remember how I was dancing round the world?'

He said, 'Yes. Summer seasons in Fayyum.' He did know really, after all.

'Ha ha, ho ho,' I went, and I was a little afraid again for if he knew me so well then surely he couldn't love me very much. Oh, how I hate feeling humble. Time to fight back. I said: 'I'm glad I didn't marry a successful man. How boring it would have been. As it is, I have had every chance to discover my own potential.

'You've always been the same, Lili,' said Robert in that gentle voice.

38

I sat in the car wondering why he'd married me. He must have loved me. I'd make him love me again. Or perhaps he still did? He was faithful to me and that must mean he loved me. But of *course* he loved me. Silly Lili.

*

As soon as we arrived at the gallery I took an intelligent interest in the exhibition. I spoke of framing and hanging and lighting, about all of which I did not know a damn thing and cared less. I was bored by painting and seldom even looked at Robert's pictures. I always said how beautiful they were but I'd never really looked at them. They were something Robert did when he wasn't with me. If he'd been an accountant I wouldn't have had to pay huge attention to his columns of figures, would I? How could I constantly be throwing myself about in transports at the glory of his paintings? I always said all the right things and I helped sell his work. I did. I made people drink a lot and buy it. Now I made several very pertinent and clever remarks and a few suggestions to which nobody listened. The hell with you – I thought – if you won't even listen to me.

We left for the restaurant; Margaret, whom I'd almost forgotten, trailing behind, and me between two silent men, both of whom, for whatever reason, were in something of a rage. I myself began to feel angry. The gallery owner was obviously regretting having agreed to exhibit my husband's paintings and I may as well confess now, for otherwise you will miss some of the complexities of the situation, that, yes, I had had the teeniest fling with this man some years before when he was first wondering whether it was worth taking Robert on. I had helped him make up his mind. A misunderstanding had arisen when he had considered that the fling should be resumed and I could see no good reason why it should. You must see my viewpoint. He had telephoned me at the dreadful hotel and I had been dismissive. Polite, but dismissive. I'm glad that's out in the open. I should not like Robert to know, but I am not, by nature, secretive. Both these men were now unjustly annoyed with me and I was fed up. We plodded on until I said, reflectively, that I loved to see men dancing. A dancing man, if he's doing the right dance, is incomparably sexy. Much more attractive than some sweating fool kicking a ball around. I knew neither of these conventional men would agree with me. They wouldn't understand.

The silence continued until Robert said, 'I was telling Lili she shouldn't have given up dancing.' This was infuriating, for it put him in the position of the superior male chiding his woman for making silly mistakes. All my subtle spite was wasted. I wanted to stop there and then and hit him, but I took a grip of myself and carried on jabbering rubbish in an effort to make things seem normal. They made the odd, uninterested response until I got really cross and said, 'Anyway art is only a snare and a delusion.' Even that didn't get through to Robert. He said: 'If it wasn't for art we wouldn't be about to eat.' I couldn't say what I was thinking, could I? That if it wasn't for me sleeping with Mr Money Bags here we wouldn't be about to eat, and it had fuck all to do with his stupid painting. No, I couldn't say that. The restaurant was of the Middle-Eastern sort, so I went on about Egypt instead. 'What a coincidence,' I cried, or something on those lines.

Money Bags said, 'I chose it specially to make you feel at home.' The liar. He didn't bother to sound as though he was telling the truth. It was cheap, that was all.

Margaret, I need hardly say, was of no help during these exchanges. She was unconscious of the tensions and the unseen currents. I made another effort and introduced the topic of food. Surprisingly she joined in and we had a little chat about the culinary attitudes of different nations. She, I was glad to hear, had no illusions about English food. I don't suppose she could have with her mother's cooking for example, but you can never really tell what people think is edible. Margaret was quite sensible on the subject.

I agreed with her. 'No wonder the English look so awful,' I said. Robert said, 'Margaret doesn't look awful.' What? What have we here? My stern husband complimenting the *petite anglaise*? What was happening? I was half English myself, after all. I said that *we* had the sense to make some effort to eat properly and maintain our looks. I meant me.

I felt lost. Not really English, not really Egyptian, not really human sometimes. Just a collection of bones and flesh that somebody once had danced in. I'm only a tutu – I thought, and sat speechless while Robert and Money Bags argued, in a disguised sort of way, about the meaning of art. It was boring.

*

I was more worried about Robert than I cared to admit. I couldn't stop thinking about it. He had wanted children. We never now talked about him wanting children. I couldn't have any. It was too late now, but I never could have had any. I'd been ill...well, something had gone wrong...well, I can't talk about it. It wasn't my fault. Not altogether. I'd been unlucky. I didn't like children anyway. They would've spoilt our life together. How can you travel and be free with a lot of screaming children? I had no regrets.

Still, I worried. I had to talk to someone. I couldn't go through all my life with no one to talk to, and I couldn't talk to Robert. Not at the moment. There was something wrong. I talked to Margaret, for it was rather like talking to yourself, and if she did respond I sometimes had the feeling that perhaps she knew what I was talking about. This is a soothing feeling when you are used only to the sort of people you meet at the club who

42

wouldn't understand a word you were saying if you spelt it out in capital letters. She never said much, but I didn't mind. If you're pouring out your soul you don't want other people pouring out theirs. There'd be a flood. Oh, I was full of grief. I don't know why. Perhaps it was the cold of Croydon, although I'd been no happier in the heat of the Nile. I had no reason to feel so sad and I thought and thought about it and finally found that I was lonely. Lonely Lili. What an absurd conception. I had never had to be lonely in all my life. There were people everywhere; people who loved me. Hundreds of people who loved me. I only had to walk to the corner of the street and smile in a way I had and I would bring back several people who, in that moment, had learned to love me. It's true.

So why was I so sad? Empty and cold and sad. I thought sometimes that I had been loved too much – not only by all those lovers, and yes, I admit there had been several; well more than that. I don't care to count because the numbers make me seem trivial and undiscerning – oh, all right, promiscuous. But I wasn't really promiscuous. I didn't like most of those men. I despised them. I knew what love was. I thought for a moment that I knew because I had never really known it; that I knew it by default as warm and real and steadfast, and I knew so well what it was like because I was cold. Not frigid, you understand. Just cold. I thought of how unthinkable it would be to betray that love. Oh hell. I did love Robert. I would never betray him – not really – but to an observer it might seem that I had. It

43

might even seem so to Robert. I hadn't meant to, not ever, only sometimes he made me so cross and then the only way I could think of to punish him was to go and be nice to somebody else. I said to myself, while Margaret listened, that we could only love once. If we loved more than once then *none* of it counted. It was all meaningless and valueless and we might as well stand under a street lamp and sell ourselves like sugar cane to whoever cared to buy. When I shut up I saw how Margaret was looking at me, and, lo, I had done it again. The little Margaret loved me. I had made no effort at all and she loved me. There. Do you see? I told you so.

I was slightly cheered. I felt suddenly sufficiently fond of her to wish that she wasn't going to marry old Syl. I could have told her then and there not to be such an ass, but Monica would have killed me, so I said in a roundabout fashion that the conventional marriage could be a rotten way to spend a lifetime. All those wedding presents getting tarnished and discoloured and curling up at the edges; a constant reminder of the death of things. But Margaret had just mentioned Mother Joseph and I grew wary. I must not let her talk of Marie Claire and Nour and her months in Egypt.

'...And did you know Sister Bridget too?' she asked. 'And the other nuns?'

'A long time ago,' I said, and, naturally, Monica chose that moment to appear. However, her invariable habit of taking a discussion off course could sometimes prove useful. She gave us her views on the selfish nature of the religious life,

44

which were of no interest to anybody but at least got us off the subject of love and marriage and away from any *faux pas* I might have made in relation to little Nour.

*

I am not as stupid as I sometimes sound. Really I'm not. I'm clever and quick and intelligent and you'd see at once what I mean if you knew me properly. I am very good with clothes. I *know* clothes. You may think this unimportant compared with the rigours of life, but clothes are not insignificant. Take Monica's wedding dress. It was bloody awful when she wore it and when she plunged her unfortunate daughter in it – well. For some reason I never could make out she was determined that the poor girl should go to her martyrdom in this appalling garment. Margaret stood on her dressing-table stool draped in the thing and I didn't know whether to laugh or to cry.

'It's lovely,' said Monica decisively. 'It just doesn't fit properly, that's all.' That wasn't all at all. It was out of date, it had never looked any good anyway, and it had dropped out of whatever shape it had ever had. Margaret looked like a badly wrapped joint.

I said I wasn't sure I could do anything with it. I tucked it and turned it and nipped it in here and there, while occasionally suggesting that we should

45

abandon the whole thing as a bad job. This didn't go down well, so I carried on pinning and changed the subject – well, almost. I was remembering my own wedding in the church of St Catherine in Alexandria, an exotic occasion with much of the English community present and also my own relations on my father's side. All the English ladies wore silk and muslin and chiffon, and so did my aunts, but some of them had insisted on wearing their furs too. I had got the giggles as we left home with my mad aunts hung about in fox and sable with the sun glaring down. I was dressed in crimson wild silk with a wreath of crimson rosebuds on my head. Monica had expressed her opinion that people with red hair shouldn't wear crimson, especially not when they were getting married, but she was wrong as usual. I looked *wonderful*. Mind you, I shouldn't have said so while I was fiddling with that frock on poor Margaret. Monica wasn't pleased. She thought I was showing off and making odious comparisons. I was.

*

She went to bed early that night and I thought if Margaret went too I could spend the evening just with Robert and a bottle of Monica's Scotch. I could make him laugh and get him a bit drunk and then...but, no. He said he was going to walk to the pub because he fancied a pint of English ale. I was

46

disappointed. I said, 'Since you'll be passing Syl's house why don't you pop in and ask him out for a drink.' Robert never could stand Syl. I'm sure he had no idea that – well, never mind. He simply couldn't stand the sight of him.

'If you ask him very prettily,' I said, 'perhaps he'll play you a tune on his flute. I had put Robert in a difficult position. He could hardly say, in front of Margaret, that he'd rather go to sea than have a drink with her fiancé. Then I looked at Margaret and felt a little guilty. She was blushing with embarrassment for, as I've already said, she wasn't stupid. She knew how Syl stood in the eyes of his contemporaries, and I was sure that her own generation would find him ridiculous. Robert had noticed too and gave me a highly critical look as he left. Oh damn, damn, damn.

Margaret suddenly said: 'Oh Lili.' And I felt sorry for her. Truly. She looked desperate. But I had bigger worries on my mind. Every time I opened my mouth it seemed I offended Robert. I was only teasing him. He should have taken *me* to the pub. I hoped he had called in at Syl's. I hoped Syl would spend the evening clinging to him like a leech. I was furious.

Then I looked at Margaret properly. Her face was so sad. She looked as sad as me – sadder. I said: 'Margaret, sometimes there are things you think you have to do but often those very things are things you must not do. Sometimes you must grow up and when people tell you you *must* do things – that's when you absolutely must *not*.' *I* could talk. I

47

was beginning to think I'd never grow up myself.

'What shall I do?' said Margaret. 'I'm stupid.'

'No, you're not,' I said. 'You've got no faith in yourself, so you've lost hope. And all I know is, if you hang on long enough hope comes back.' I hoped I was right. My own hope was shaky tonight.

'But I've *got* to go through with it now,' said Margaret. The poor little animal had admitted, without even realising, that her marriage approached as might her doom. Oh well. How could she have been so idiotic as to let matters go this far?

I lost patience with her. I went to bed.

*

The next day Syl came round, all dressed up as lamb. 'Why Syl,' I said, 'how young you look. How very young and carefree.' He believed me. He smiled. He was stupid to believe me and I was angry, for it made me feel wicked: wicked and spiteful and rather old and too clever by half. Grown-up people should understand the rules of the game; should know when one is telling tiny lies and being a tiny bit cruel. They should respond in kind. Syl should have said: 'And you, Lili, you too are as fresh and lovely as once you were.' Or something like that. Something polished and untrue and sociable, and then the game could have continued as a pleasant little contest between

48

equals. As it was, all my barbs were wasted and I thought I must sound gushing and ordinary. I thought I might as well go on like that since there was no fun to be had. I turned to Monica and struck up a conventional conversation about her house. At least I *meant* it to be conventional but she grew pompous about it and the devil got back into me. 'Why don't you sell it?' I said after she'd given a sort of lecture on the place. 'It's far too big for you and you'd probably get a lot of money for it.' Monica had that effect on me. She made me want to say vulgar things and I knew she thought there was nothing more vulgar than talking about money. She did look insulted so I added that she was probably right not to sell – the house might have been made for her. It wasn't really a compliment, but she took it as such. So that was all right.

Syl joined in, saying that now was not the time to sell. Margaret left the room as he spoke and I wondered if they'd noticed. I noticed everything. If you want to survive you have to. I told Monica that my own house badly needed painting and the wind had taken all the shine from the stonework. She gave me some advice on the matter and we were friends again. 'Where's Margaret gone?' asked Syl. It was a bit late but he had noticed.

'I think she went into the garden,' said Monica. 'Run out and find her,' Syl got up in what I suppose he thought was a lithe bound and went off in pursuit of his affianced. I waited for Monica to say something like 'Oh, he's so devoted', but she didn't.

Even Monica couldn't keep up a pretence *all* the time. She said she was going to pick some autumn leaves to brighten the hallway and I asked myself if she was intending to spy on Margaret and see how she behaved to Syl; check that her daughter wasn't ruining her chances by being impolite or remote or cheeky to her old suitor. I had a vision of Monica bobbing up from behind a hedge saying 'Margaret, apologise at once' or 'Take no notice of her, Syl. She's just being silly.' It wasn't impossible. Monica was a terrible worrier and worriers can't help interfering. They think if they meddle they won't have to worry so much. Oh, how mistaken they are. Margaret reappeared in the sitting room. It was getting rather like French farce without the bedroom scenes. 'Where is everyone?' I asked. 'I thought you were all in the garden?' Margaret didn't answer. She'd torn off a hangnail and there was blood dripping everywhere – all over her frock. I hate to see clothes being spoiled. What a messy girl she was. I took her out to the tap and cleaned her up.

'What's going on?' asked Monica suspiciously, appearing at the door. Did she think I'd attacked her child?

'Nothing, nothing,' I said. 'She bit her thumb.'

'She'll probably get blood-poisoning,' said Monica unhelpfully. She didn't really sound as though she cared. I asked where she kept the bandages but she was too busy arranging her autumn leaves to answer me. There were tears in Margaret's eyes, so I started talking a lot. Don't misunderstand me. I'm not afraid of scenes. I just didn't think that was the time for one. At least one person should be drunk when there's a scene, because then everyone can pretend that it didn't happen, or if it did there was a good excuse and reconciliations are unnecessary. A sober scene in the cold light of day can lead to all manner of unfortunate results. Often the bystander gets the blame. Monica could easily have blamed me – for making too much fuss, for encouraging Margaret to be feeble and self-pitying, for being there at all.

'There's no need to cry,' said Monica who seemed bent on trouble.

'She's not *crying*,' I said. 'It was cold out there in the garden, wasn't it, Margaret? It made her nose red, that's all.' I thought that Margaret must have been distant with Syl and Monica had overheard. 'You should see *me* cry,' I said. 'Then you'd know what crying really was.' 'What have *you* got to cry about?' asked Monica rudely. She was the most insensitive woman I'd ever met and I couldn't think why I'd ever bothered with her at all. OK, Monica – I thought – pin your ears back.

I said: 'Sometimes I sink into a grand black horror of depression, but I don't cry so much then. I stay in bed and pluck at the counterpane and listen to the winds of solitude roaring at the edge of infinity and the wolves of evil baying down the void, and I look into the darkness.' There, Monica – I thought – see what you can do with that one.

'Oh, don't be so morbid, Lili,' she said. 'Try and say something cheerful.'

51

It was a waste of time getting clever with Monica. 'I can't think of anything cheerful,' I said. 'Can you?'

Monica rallied. 'Well, the wedding of *course*,' she said. God, what a stupid woman. She didn't leave it at that. 'It'll be such fun,' she said. I didn't say anything. I was sick of wasting my breath; so Monica went on to describe the awful old wedding menu. She recited it.

'*And* speeches,' I said. '*And* confetti. *And* warm champagne.' I could imagine the whole thing. There was something uniquely dreadful about English weddings. I'd been to dozens of the horrible occasions. Oh, they weren't all so bad, I suppose. Just most of them. They made me think of death, perhaps because there was no music and no dancing. No Zâgharit.

'What's wrong with confetti?' asked Monica aggressively.

'Nothing,' I said. 'Nothing. I just don't like weddings much.'

'You seemed to enjoy your own,' said Monica. I glanced at Margaret but I don't think she was listening. I didn't want to go into details about my wedding. I had enjoyed it – what I could remember of it. It had been all right. I'd asked Robert and he'd laughed and said I'd been all right. 'I should have had a gypsy wedding,' I said. 'I should have jumped over the flames in the darkness of the night.'

'You might have burnt your red frock,' said Monica.

'Robert would have rescued me,' I said, 'stamped out the embers ind raced with me into the trees.'

'Robert would have turned the fire extinguisher on you,' said Monica. Oops, Monica had that disconcerting way of the very thick of sometimes saying something accurate. Something that hit the nail on the head. That was just what Robert would have done. He had adored me but he had always been sensible. Change the subject. Get Robert out of it.

'I might have married a gypsy,' I said. 'Spotted scarf. Gold earrings.'

Monica wouldn't let it go. 'I thought Robert was the only man in the world for you,' she said. I thought that rather brutal of her considering how well she knew me – not *me* exactly, but she knew more than I liked about what could be described as my Past.

'He is,' I said sincerely. 'I was only fantasising.' I thought this was a generous concession and should be left untouched but Monica took advantage of it. Bitch. 'You do too much of that,' she said.

Right – I thought – you want to fight dirty. OK. I said in a sweet voice: 'When is Derek coming?' Monica hated him. I knew how much she hated him because I'd been there when she started to. We'd stayed with them here at the time Derek was beginning to play around, and even before that, when they were in Egypt, she'd begun to notice him edging his way towards girls. He liked them young. A thought struck me...

'They're arriving the night before the wedding,' Monica informed me coldly.

53

I was thinking about Syl. He liked them young too. Poor Margaret. Her life was full of old men who liked them young.

'No stag night for Syl?' I asked. 'Of course not,' said Monica. I was tired of trying to be tactful. 'I suppose he is a bit old for that sort of thing,' I said.

Margaret went red and I felt sorry for her again, but Monica didn't say anything. Not to me. She knew she'd met her match in me, so she started bullying Margaret.

*

I had to get out of the house quite often now. Never mind the cold. I was fond of Monica. I was. I always had been but she was impossible in her present mood. Bossy and martyred and *impossible*. It was because she knew she was in the wrong. It was really *very* wrong of her to make Margaret marry Syl, and that was what she was doing. It was obvious. I was amazed that everyone couldn't see it. She knew it but she told herself she was doing the right thing.

'Robert,' I said, as we drove one morning towards Tottenham Court Road, 'what do you think of Margaret?'

'Abishag the Shulamite?' he said.

'Who?' I said.

'You're an ignorant savage, Lili,' he said, for he was feeling fond of me that day. His evil mood had

54

passed. In view of this I let him explain about the girl who was chosen to keep the ancient David warm. One of those dubious Bible stories that they didn't read to us in school. I knew it anyway. I laughed.

Robert laughed too. I wondered for a moment *why* he was in such an agreeable frame of mind. I could see no particular reason for it. 'What's she doing, marrying Syl?' he asked. It wasn't the sort of thing he was usually interested in – human relationships seldom attracted his attention.

'Monica's making her,' I said.

'Nonsense,' said Robert.

'*Robert*,' I said, hoping he wasn't going to annoy me.

'I can see she's in favour of it,' said Robert, 'but she can hardly force her into it.'

'Can't she?' I said.

'How could she?' said Robert.

I wondered how I could begin to explain to him how people make people do things. I wondered why he needed an explanation. He could make me do things by withdrawing his approval. Often he made me do things he wouldn't approve of by disapproving of me in the first place. Mostly I liked to please him but I have my pride.

'Abishag the Shulamite hasn't got my pride,' I said.

'Just a hot water bottle,' said Robert.

That wasn't what I meant. Not quite. I meant she did what she was told because she had no proper image of herself.

'She has no self-respect,' I said and for some reason Robert laughed again. Why *was* he so cheerful?

*

Robert had to go and see his solicitor about something. I asked him why he didn't use Syl as his man of business and he told me not to be funny. I spent the afternoon in the Colony Rooms with the painters and the writers and the riff-raff, and my friend Celestine, who had a flat in Bramerton Street. Robert picked me up there but he wouldn't stay. It may have been because famous painters went there and Robert wasn't famous. Not yet. I kissed Celestine goodbye and she winked at me. I had borrowed her spare key. She was out most days and sometimes it was nice to have somewhere to go where I could just put my feet up and not have to be polite to anyone. It was a bit dusty, but so what.

If I wasn't in Monica's house for too long it was a pleasant contrast to the noise and the dust and the paint of the painters. Nice to go home in the evenings and sit in the chintz. No dust. Monica didn't like dust. I couldn't have lived with all that dust for long either, but nor could I have lived forever with all that chintz. Perhaps that was why I was a wanderer. Dirt and grease one minute, shampoo and bath salts the next. Variety.

Monica was still fussing about the wedding dress.

I could have done with a little sleep when we got back but duty called. I managed to sew Margaret into the damn thing. I tacked it to her *chemise* and she got quite upset when she couldn't get out of it. I once sewed a whole skirt seam to a table cover and it *is* annoying, but Margaret made nearly as much fuss as her mother. I was surprised. She said she needed a drink and Monica snapped at her. I was soothing.

'She's got some way to go before she's an alcoholic,' I said. 'She's not like me.'

'Oh nonsense,' said Monica. God, she was irritating. I couldn't even claim to drink too much without being contradicted.

'Don't you worry about my liver?' I asked pitifully. 'Don't you believe me?'

'I've got better things to worry about,' said Monica. She spoke to Margaret: 'Don't forget you're having tea with Syl's mother tomorrow.'

Syl's mother. Yes. I was going to have to think about Syl's mother. There could be a certain awkwardness....

'Robert will be getting lonely,' I said. 'Down there all by himself.'

'We'll go down now,' said Monica, folding up the dress. She grumbled fitfully as she did so. All about a poor woman on her own and the responsibility of arranging a wedding; the organisation, the cost, the wear and tear on the nerves. She turned on Margaret and started nagging her – where was her ring? What about her trousseau? Had she done this? Had she done that? Margaret didn't say anything but I could feel the tension in her. 'You're a lump,' said her mother. 'You don't seem to enjoy anything.' I did so wish she'd shut up. You can push the meekest little mouse too far, and I needed a peaceful evening. I didn't want Robert bothered with all this bad temper and emotion. He'd only blame me.

'She could've got her clothes in Cairo,' I said trying to change the subject again. It was like trying to haul a mule down an alley when it's got its feet splayed.

'She wouldn't think of *that*,' said Monica, implying that Margaret wouldn't think of anything useful.

'But on the other hand,' I said, 'she didn't know she was going to get married then.' I was beginning to feel hysterical. Monica ignored me. 'Why aren't you seeing Syl tonight?' she demanded of Margaret.

'He's going out,' said Margaret without interest.

Monica lost her temper. She shouted. Well, not loudly, but it *was* a shout. 'Don't you love Syl?' Oh boy – I thought – here we go. Take cover. Margaret's going to tell the truth. But she didn't. She said, of course she loved Syl.

I was so relieved I let out my breath. 'Love?' I said. 'What's that?' I had to say something but I wished I'd thought of something else, for Monica turned on me now. Yes, I know it was a stupid remark, but you haven't experienced the atmosphere Monica could create. It addled your brains.

'I thought *you* were the expert,' she said, quick as a whiplash.

Ouch. 'Who me?' I said. 'Not me. I know nothing

58

at all about it.' I wish I could describe the look
Monica gave me. I can't. Anyway we went
downstairs then and Monica behaved herself
because of Robert, and we drank a lot and went to
bed. Whew.

*

Yes. Syl's mother. Hmmm. Here was a tricky one.
It was some years now but she had reason to be –
well, displeased with me. Yes. All right. If I arrived
at her house she had every reason to throw me out.
I'd have to see her sooner or later. I thought I
might as well go with Margaret and get it over with.
If there was going to be a scene it had better not be
at the wedding. *Courage, mon brave*. Smart frock.
Lots of lipstick. Big smile.
    Margaret rang the doorbell and the dog barked.
I reflected that I'd sooner be paddling in the
crocodile pool. Door opened. '*Hullo*,' I said, full of
enthusiasm. No point in seeming apologetic.
    I was inside. I was sitting down. She hadn't been
pleased to see me but she hadn't pointed an
accusing finger and ordered me off her doorstep. I
certainly didn't feel at ease, but nor did she, poor
old trout. She went back and forth carrying cakes
and teapots. I smoked like a mad thing and
jabbered to the dog and nobody else said a word
until she scolded Margaret for not eating up her
tea. She went off again to get more hot water and I

59

whispered to Margaret that she should tell her to boil her head.

Margaret said, 'Sshhh', and I lit another cigarette. I was so nervous. The dog was sitting on my foot and I kicked him off – quite gently, but he yelped.

'What are you doing to the dog?' asked Syl's mother who had to pick that moment to come back.

Do you know what I said? Do you know what the devil put it into my head to say? I said the dog was fucking my foot. That's what I said. I wished I could die then and there – slap, face down in the sandwiches. Why, of everything in the world I could have said, did I have to say that? Of all the subjects in the world I had to choose that one. Oh *God*. The last time she'd seen me I was doing that with her husband in Monica's summer-house at the bottom of the garden – *flagrante delicto*. I hadn't been going to mention it. Well, *of course* I wasn't going to mention it. Oh *dear* God. I considered getting on the window seat and throwing myself out through the glass, but she didn't seem to mind.

She said, perfectly calmly, 'He's not capable of that', and for a second I wondered dementedly if she was talking of her husband. He hadn't really been... *Shut up, Lili*.

I said, 'Well, he was thinking about it', amazed that I could speak at all – never mind sound quite composed.

'You can read the minds of animals?' asked Syl's mother, and I wondered if she'd forgotten. Forgotten what I was doing the last time she saw me. I gabbled like a lunatic. God knows what I said but I went on saying it without thinking until I heard myself saying that the dog had simply been overwhelmed by *lust*. I couldn't seem to leave it alone. I suppose some shrink would say it was guilt. Maybe it was. Whatever it was I have never felt such a fool in my life. Oh how I wished I'd died on the doorstep. Oh Lili, how *could* you?

'He's old,' said Syl's mother.

She was still perfectly calm, and I began to pull myself together. I began to talk very, very carefully about travelling, about Egypt, about Tutankhamun, about anything that had nothing whatsoever to do with sex. I was very boring but at least I never mentioned fucking again. Oh *Lili*.

*

It was cold outside, thank God. I'd been sweating. I have never been so embarrassed ever. And mixed up with all that was a sort of gratitude to Syl's mother. She had taken it very well. The worst thing was I'd always rather liked her. I'd pretended not to because nobody else liked her and it hadn't seemed worth being contrary at the time. There were plenty of other things to be contrary about. When she'd caught me with her husband in the summer house I'd disliked her because I'd wronged her, but as the memory faded I remembered her, when I remembered her at all, as

61

different from and better than all the other silly
English ladies. I had absolutely meant to pretend
that the little *contretemps* with what's-his-name –
Jack, I think, he was called – had never happened.
That was how we all managed. Just pretend it
never happened. It usually worked fairly well. I
couldn't think what had come over me suddenly to
mind so much that I could think of nothing else.
Oh dear.

Margaret didn't seem to have noticed anything.
She walked along in silence until she asked: 'Do you
ever bore yourself?'

Bore myself? No, not often. Not today, anyway.
'Yes,' I said, 'I just did.' If she hadn't noticed
anything I wasn't going to tell her.

'You weren't boring,' she said.

'Yes I was,' I said. Much better to be boring than
what I had been. Tactless was not quite the word.

'I can never think of anything to say to her,' said
Margaret. I was growing cooler now and was so
chastened by my own performance that I felt well
disposed towards her. At the moment I had a lot of
leeway to make up in my relationship with the
human race. I was not going to be unkind to
anybody for several days. I was in no position to be.
I said it was very difficult talking to a person of a
different age from your own, a person with
different experiences. I said one could only really
talk to people who had shared one's experience
and that *gossip* was the only useful and valid form
of conversation. Why did I say that? I was highly
wary of gossip, and as to shared experience – well,

it could be said that Syl's mother and I had shared an experience, and look where it had got me.

'I wish I was like you,' said Margaret.

The girl was mad. Still, it was sweet of her. 'You are a bit,' I said kindly.

'I'm not happy like you,' she said.

Oh! I told her there wasn't any point in being unhappy. Not if you could help it. Besides I *was* happy basically; most of the time.

We walked on in silence, me breathing deeply. And then she said, 'Lili?'

'Mmmm,' I said.

'Can I tell you something?'

'What?'

'I can't tell anyone else.'

Oh hell. Girlish confidences. 'Don't tell anyone,' I said. She could put me in a hopeless position if she told me things. 'If you've got a secret you can't keep,' I said, 'you must either tell everyone or tell nobody.' I wasn't going to be held responsible for one more indiscretion. 'Tell the priest,' I said.

*

'Did you have a good time?' asked Monica. She was being sarcastic now.

'Terrific,' I said. I really needed a drink, I felt worn out what with one thing and another.

'What did you think of Mrs Monro?' asked Monica who seemed bent on tormenting me. I said

I thought she was wonderful. What was I supposed to say? I was still so annoyed with myself I couldn't really think properly. Somewhere in my mind I entertained the reflection that although she was an old lady singularly lacking in charm she was twice – no several times – the woman Monica was. I wanted to say so but of course I couldn't. I still wished she was a silly, nasty old woman because once I had behaved badly to her. I thought that behaving badly was worse than anyone knew because it distorted relationships. If you poured boiling soup over an angel it would be years before you could like or fully appreciate that angel because he had conspired in being wronged by you to put you in the wrong. Do you see what I mean?

Monica continued assessing Mrs Monro's good points without being accurate at all. She missed all the *really* good points. She said she was a good cook and would make an excellent mother-in-law. Monica was a pastmaster at saying stupid things; things to which there was no answer. I stopped listening. She didn't offer me a drink so I got one for myself. I *needed* it. And where was Robert? Tell me that.

*

Oh. He came back. Quite early. I was relieved. I was full of gladness to see him. When Lili was wicked she was lonely. Poor Lili. But when Robert

64

was there it meant he was there because he loved me, and I felt like a flower that had been picked up from the path and put in water. I did. I don't care how ridiculous it sounds.

'Hullo,' I said – very casually, because now he was there I didn't need to expand or be enthusiastic. I could relax. 'How does it look?'

'It's all right,' said Robert. He didn't sound too enthusiastic either. I felt a tiny anxiety. We couldn't afford any reversals in our fortunes.

'Do you think we should ask him to dinner?' I said *before* thinking.

Wham. Monica was on to me in a second. 'Who?' she said in a cold, demanding voice. Then Margaret put her foot in it. 'Robert's gallery owner,' she said. I could have smacked her. I'd been going to say that I meant we should take him out to the Ritz or somewhere and take Monica too. I didn't mean that at all but I was going to say I did. Robert said he wouldn't dream of asking the mean bastard to dinner and Monica – who was perverse – said that in that case perhaps she would offer him a simple meal if it would help.

Robert said there was no need. Money Bags couldn't back out of it now. I felt a little chilled to realise that Robert had seen this as a possibility. 'I wouldn't let him back out,' I said, 'I wouldn't.'

'You could hardly stop him,' said Robert. Oh, yes I could. I'd blackmail him or seduce him or hold him at gun point or sit on his head until he agreed to make Robert rich and famous. I wouldn't let him get away with it. I needed Robert to look after me.

Perhaps that's why I would have killed to protect him. Love is a peculiar thing. I don't understand it altogether but I can follow its little breadcrumbs of clues for quite a long way. They go round and round and round. Robert was my mother and my child and without him I was desolate. Without him I would be dead.

*

He went out. Brute. OK – I thought – so go out without me. See if I care. I've had millions of lovers and I don't need *you*. I talked about them in a disguised sort of way, just to let Monica and Margaret know that I didn't need to depend on any one man. You could say it was bravado. Perhaps it was, but I had to survive. I remembered being in love lots of times, and it was like madness because one day you return to your senses and you think – what was all that about? And you look at your lover who you loved so much and you can't imagine *why*. I must have been mad – you say to yourself, and you shake your head to clear it, and you wish quite passionately that you hadn't let anyone see how much you loved him, and you muddy the waters by pretending to love someone else now, and you laugh lightly at the mention of his name. Oh *him* – you say. I'd forgotten about *him*.

Monica didn't want to talk about lovers because she hadn't got any. Margaret was thinking about

66

something else, so I let my talking slow down and drift away. They went to bed and I sat and waited for my husband to come back.

*

He hadn't been out long. He'd gone to the pub, silly man. When he came back he didn't talk to me. He went to sleep, and after a long while I went to sleep too.

The next day I got bored with Monica wondering whether the fish was fresh and talking about it, and I said I would go for a little walk. I went behind the gardens to see Syl's mother. I don't know *quite* why I did that. I couldn't apologise to her because it had not been generally acknowledged that I'd done anything amiss. Do you know – I think I went simply because I wanted to. Because I *liked* her. Yes, I did still feel very bad about what I'd said and, yes, I did sort of want to make amends – without doing anything so embarrassing as saying I was sorry – but mostly I just wanted to go and see her. She made such a change from Monica and Margaret. Like strong cheese and pickles after pudding – if you see what I mean. She wasn't stupid. It was such a *relief*.

Besides I could talk to her and sometimes I needed to talk. I never really meant to tell her anything important but I could talk to her about real proper things. Naturally I found myself

67

talking about Robert. I talked about the past too. I don't know why I was always talking about the past these days. And death. Why did I talk about death? That wasn't very tactful either when you consider the age of Syl's mother. I was obviously a little run-down. What I said was that you could have enough of life. I was thinking about meals. All those meals one had eaten – mostly just to keep alive. But some of the better ones had been too much. For instance it was hard to eat a whole lobster. A little delicious bit of lobster was enough. And lamb. Nobody could eat a whole lamb. I sometimes felt that just a little bit of delicious life would be preferable to platefuls and platefuls of it – stretching away into the future forever. The thought gave me indigestion. And I didn't want to find myself, one day, as old as Syl's mother. Oh no. I would settle for the merest *hors d'oeuvres* of life rather than chew through to that stage. I didn't tell her so. I almost told her how I couldn't have children, but that was because I was feeling guilty about it. I had never felt guilty about it when I was younger. Only now when I was getting older ... Not very guilty. It was only one more small thing to worry about sometimes – in the night when Robert was asleep. Later we went into London. I was feeling full of pride – hurt pride if you like. Nobody was going to treat me like that and get away with it. No, never. I told Robert to drop me in Sloane Square and I walked down to Celestine's place. I had a few phone calls to make. Well, one in particular. Celestine was there but she was just going out. She stayed a bit longer when I arrived because she liked my company. I made her laugh. We drank some very strong coffee out of dirty mugs. She'd run them under the tap but the lipstick hadn't come off. She looked at her watch and said she must fly. When she got to the doorway she stopped to utter an afterthought. 'Oh,' she said, 'Lili, if you'd just remember to change the sheets.' Even the dirtiest girl can be fussy about some things. I said I would before I remembered that I hadn't told her that the need would arise. Oh well. Never mind. I didn't have to keep secrets from Celestine because she could keep her mouth shut. Her own life was sufficiently exciting without her having to gab about mine. She was quite unlike Monica.

So the day passed as I had intended, which was satisfactory. Not the best day of my life admittedly but at least I was in control. My arrangements had worked without a flaw and afterwards I said: 'You must go now or you'll be late getting back to work. I'll ring you when I'm here again, or I'll drop in a note with a cryptic message. Goodbye darling...' I said, '...give me a kiss.'

I should not have done what I had just done, but it wasn't important. Robert had made me angry. Robert had made me feel unwanted. What I had just done served Robert right. Hadn't done anyone any harm. Just made me feel better. A bit better. A very little bit. Oh, God.

Then I tidied up Celestine's place and went shopping. I went to Fortnum's because I felt at home there. I always had. When we were rich I don't think my aunts knew that there was anywhere else to shop in the whole of London – except for Harrods of course – but it was Fortnums they liked best. I bought some cheese for Monica and made the man behind the counter fall in love with me just to show that I could. I kept meaning to stop doing that sort of thing because it could lead to trouble but it was quite hard to resist. Sometimes I felt I would disappear if I couldn't see the person opposite falling in love with me. I just wouldn't be there. Now, however, I felt tranquil because I was in charge and I had proved that I only had to snap my fingers and – lo ...

I felt pleased with myself all the way to the French pub where I was meeting Robert. I could feel the little lines of tiredness and sorrow had gone from my face, and when the taxi driver fell in love with me too I felt quite complete.

'Hi there, husband,' I said, 'how've you been?' Robert didn't like what he called my Americanisms.

'Oh, there you are darling,' he said and I saw that he too looked rested and fulfilled.

'Oh gee,' I said, 'gimme a drink, and fast', for I was suddenly terribly angry. What had made the bastard look so well and so young, and so pleased with himself? *What?* Answer me that.

'I did such a good deal today,' he said.

'Deal?' I said.

'A *good* deal,' he said. 'My brother began it and I finished it ...'

Oh God. He'd been doing a deal and I'd thought

70

... oh never mind what I'd thought. Oh *God*. Lili, you are such a silly bitch sometimes.

I threw a drink down my throat and I said, 'Tell me about it.' I lit a cigarette and my hands were trembling. Their grandfather had left them some old pictures and books and things and Robert's brother had taken them to a dealer and been offered a thousand pounds, so Robert had gone and seen this dealer and told him to jump in the lake, and he'd taken away the pictures and books and sold them to two different dealers for five thousand pounds. That was very clever. I was very pleased. I said so. What I didn't say was that if the stupid man had told me that that was what he was doing then I wouldn't have been doing what I'd been doing. Not necessarily, anyway. No, I *wouldn't*. It was all Robert's fault.

'Why didn't you tell me before?' I asked. I knew why. Robert told me what I already knew. 'I didn't want to disappoint you if nothing came of it.'

'I see,' I said. 'Let's have another drink to celebrate.'

'You don't sound very pleased,' said Robert.

'I am pleased,' I said. 'I'm *very* pleased.'

'Well, you don't sound it,' said Robert.

'Well, I am,' I said. You can see what was likely to happen next, can't you? A screaming row in the French pub because my husband had made me feel guilty. I felt a fool too, which was worse. Oh, *bugger*.

'Let's go home,' I said. Home. Where was home? Home was where Robert was. What would I do if I lost him? Oh, be quiet Lili. How could you lose him?

71

In the car I spoke unnaturally of how clever I thought he'd been.

'You needn't go on, Lili,' he said, as though I was a stranger.

I began to say again: 'But I mean it ...' and stopped. I was silent until we got back and he was silent too. Misunderstanding is the worst thing in the world.

*

There was plenty of misunderstanding in Monica's house. I could sense it in the air. I was tired now but I had to take the stage again. Dash of lipstick. Big smile. Never mind the aching feet. The best thing I could do, I thought, was to talk about the past. The dead old past tucked away with the dried oleander petals, juiceless and inoffensive now.

'Do you remember ...?' I began.

'I remember ...' said Monica. She remembered different things from me. She remembered in different ways. She was talking about going to the tennis club in the school holdiays while I was remembering watching an aunt mash up Spanish Fly to put in a jar of mutton grease – the dark shuttered room, the smell of rancid nard and attar of roses, and me not understanding what she was doing or why. I know *now* what she was doing and why, but I didn't know then. She was making a love potion for external application to somebody's straying husband. I don't know why I was thinking about that. It wasn't as though I needed any ointment for a dying desire. I was tired, that was all.

Margaret too seemed to have a different sort of memory from her mother. For one thing she seemed to have liked the people whereas I don't suppose Monica ever noticed them except as a sort of decoration to go with the camels and the pyramids and the palm trees. But then if Margaret had been in love with Nour she would have a different conception of his land. She would have been in love with his land too. Poor little mouse. Whenever my confidence is at a low ebb I begin to feel sorry for other people. A debilitating sense of pity creeps between my bones, making me imperfect and weak. I wondered what had happened in Egypt to give rise to the fuss that Marie Claire had made. She had flown into hysterics and accused Margaret *in absentia* of all manner of indelicacy and even criminal behaviour. It had been quite impossible to get at the truth – even to discover if there was any significant truth to be got at. There had been rumours all over the village. Rumours of sex and even murder – but you know what villages are like. I'd talked to Mother Joseph about it and she said it was all nonsense. She said they were saying that Margaret and Nour had killed a beggar girl who had appeared from nowhere one day. But – said Mother Joseph – she had herself sent away that same beggar girl from the convent gate where she was trying to sell what

73

she shouldn't be selling days after the time when this reported killing had taken place. I thought it more probable – improbable though it was – that Nour had suggested marrying Margaret. That would have been enough to send his mother into fits. If her precious Nour was going to marry anybody he was going to marry an heiress, restore the family fortunes and keep Marie Claire in her accustomed luxury. Not marry an English mouse with no money. It was not impossible that Nour had fallen a little in love with Margaret. Her cold fairness would have held an appeal for him, I know. What I couldn't quite see was why Mother Joseph held Margaret in such high esteem. She really did. I'd been surprised, for she was not one for enthusiasm. I'd known her since I was a little girl and she was seldom enthusiastic. Not even about me. No. I'm joking. I didn't mind that. I didn't mind her talking about Margaret with such interest and fondness. No. I just found it puzzling. It made it seem that there was more to Margaret than met the eye and I couldn't for the life of me think what it could be. You know how annoying that feeling is – that there's something going on that you don't understand. I couldn't make it out at all. Margaret, in fact, *was* a bit of a mystery. Why, for instance, was she going to marry Syl? I know I keep going on about it, but I really couldn't understand it and it made me cross. Syl I could understand. I knew him quite well after all. I knew he'd always been chasing young girls and I thought perhaps I knew why. His father had been the same.

74

One day I had remembered a conversation I'd had with Syl's mother, years ago, before – well before the *contretemps* – when I had wondered aloud why Syl was such an undefatigable runner-after of girls. I was really curious about his father, but I couldn't say that, could I? I was no angel, I know, but Syl and his papa left me standing. To be honest, his mother seemed as puzzled as I was. Oddly, she was not averse to talking about it. Perhaps she wanted to talk about it because it worried her and she needed to get it out of her mind. We never did reach any conclusions and I couldn't tell her what I was thinking because it wasn't the sort of thing you can tell a mother. At its simplest it is that promiscuous men are bad lovers. I don't want to go into details but it's true. If you think about it you'll find you agree with me. That is, of course, if you have had the poor sense to experiment with a promiscuous man. Yes, I know, I did, but I had reasons of my own. For one brief moment when I was run down I had been in love with him. It didn't last but I got to know him rather well – *very* well. But as I was saying – the fact is that too much practice makes for staleness. There is a brisk professionalism about the business. You feel that somewhere he keeps a well-thumbed handbook of technique and goes through the motions by rote. Yes. The skill is the skill of the club professional and lacks spontaneity. Almost it is like something that they do for a living and not for love. It is dispiriting. Also they tend to give instructions – do this, do that – and this is insulting. You come away wondering whether his salary will cover the effort or if you should perhaps leave a tip. May heaven preserve me from being the female of this species. What an awful thought. I am not speaking of prostitution. It is something else. Something more depressing because it is unexpected. Oh Lord. I had not slept with Syl for the right reason. By the time I slept with him I was no longer in love with him. Partly it was competitiveness – anything you can do I can do better – and partly it was my most usual reason – to get even with Robert for being mean to me. *Lousy* reasons. I felt positively ashamed of myself. Yes, I did, and now I'd gone and done it again. Aah, let me think of something else.

*

Once upon a time I had owned a pair of bright green chiffon pyjamas – evening ones, not the sort English men sleep in. I wore very high-heeled soft leather shoes with them. Bright green and tan shoes. They nearly killed me. I danced with the King and he told me how he'd mended the clock in the *Hotel de Ville* with his own hands. It's *true*. But he really liked English ladies – big fat fair ones – so we didn't get on all that well. I didn't mind. I didn't find him attractive but he was quite pleasant to talk to. This had all happened years ago in Alexandria before it was spoilt. Monica was there in a velvet kind of wrap with feathers. I could even remember what we had to eat. French food – cold fish and sauces, and chickens and sauces, and salads. I took my shoes off when I sat down on a little gold chair to eat. I left them off to walk home because they wouldn't go on again. Monica – or maybe it wasn't Monica – maybe it was somebody else since they are much of a muchness, these English ladies – said I couldn't possibly walk home, and certainly not without shoes, but I like to go barefoot in the soft subtle dust of the streets. The dirt that God washed off the people's feet was not the dirt of your English sweaty socks but the dirt of the earth. It drifted up past one's ankles and it was a pleasure to wash it off in a bowl of cool water. Do you see? Monica didn't. Monica couldn't really see anything. She didn't like the dirt and she didn't like the heat and she couldn't eat the food. She was quite complimentary about the bay shining under the moon and she thought my monkey was sweet if he kept at a distance and didn't put date stones in her hair, but she didn't think a lot of the pyramids and she absolutely despised Egyptian driving. I rather enjoyed it. There is something exhilarating about a mass of cars and lorries and mules and camels bearing down on you if you get out of the way in time. I like to live dangerously. Mind you, I had been careful with the men. The city was easy-going then and all the English were flirting with each other all the time, but my Dada was an Oriental and it gets into you – the feeling that unchastity deserves death. I never felt really relaxed doing the

77

flirting in Egypt. Once, you see, there was a Sultana who strayed. She must have been completely mad – or perhaps she was English and had been captured by Barbary pirates as a *cadeau* for the King – for she had her little adventure in the palace garden, up against a cypress tree. The sultan was looking for her for hours, which was bad luck since he had three more wives and three hundred concubines and probably hadn't given her a thought in weeks. So there he was scouring the rooms and balconies and terraces, bending down to look under the divans and behind the jasmine, and all the soldiers of the guard and the eunuchs, black and white, were scuttling round calling 'Cooee' and they *couldn't* find her. Don't ask me why when she was leaning against that cypress all the time. Then when she was finally discovered the Sultan couldn't see the face of her lover, who had prudently done the marathon down the garden path. *But* he had seen the device which the lover wore emblazoned on the back of his cloak and knew by that to which family he belonged. With the cruel guile of the offended potentate he invited all the men of this family to partake of a glass of mint tea, and when they gathered in a little room he called the executioner and his apprentices, and thirty-five heads rolled in the pool in the middle of the floor where the plashing of the fountain cooled the air and pleased the senses. When I was a little girl I used to think what an awful tea-party that must have been. I hated tea-parties anyway. When I grew older I asked what had happened to the

Sultana. Oh – said my aunts – she was *repudiated*.
Such a dreadful word. It sounded dreadful when I
didn't know what it meant and just as dreadful
when I did. Worse. Pish – said my aunts, waving a
hand dismissively – she was repudiated. No one
spoke to her, no one looked at her, they threw her
the crusts the doves had left until she died. A living
ghost until death took her. Think how pleased the
other wives would have been. Picture the vengeful
mirth of the concubines. The wives had their own
apartments and the principal wife had the best one,
while the concubines had to muddle along together
in an upstairs room behind a latticed screen, trying
to spit in the wives' sherbet, as they strolled in the
garden below, idly plucking the petals off
carnations. A bad man makes women bad. Yes, I'm
sure it works the other way too, but women are not
usually violent and cruel until some man upsets
them – then they're nasty to each other. A lot of
women have been nasty to me. I could so easily
have been that stupid Sultana.

'Oh, give me, give me a drink,' I said, 'Emfadlek.'

*

I changed into my Paris frock to cheer myself up
and I poured on some scent I may have kept
slightly too long. It was definitely just on the turn as
wine goes to vinegar. Underneath was still the
sweet smell that it started with, but overall the

79

impression was a bit putrefactive. I couldn't be bothered to bathe and wash it off so I pretended it was meant to be that way.

'What a smell,' said Monica. 'That takes me back.'

'Is it not delightful?' I said. 'Is it not erotic?'

'No,' said Monica, 'but it's terribly powerful.' She turned up her nose. How annoying. I knew I smelled odd without her telling everyone. The devil got into me again. It was all Monica's fault.

'Derek used to like it,' I said. Why on earth did I say that? Yes, I know. To upset Monica. I was in a bad mood. She didn't know what to answer and I didn't really blame her. I'd bowled her a nasty one.

'He had no sense of smell,' she said, having cast around for some crushing response and failed to find one. I relented towards her. 'No,' I said, 'he hadn't, had he? He didn't go on like the rest of you moaning about the North African odour.' I was not as polite as I might have been because Monica was a difficult woman to be polite to. To be honest I'd never really known Derek very well. He'd been one of the paler, more anonymous husbands and he'd never made a pass at me. If I had indicated that he should, of course he would have, but there was obviously absolutely nothing to be gained from a fling with Derek. No fun, no envy; nothing but making Monica cross, and if I wanted to do that there were a million less drastic ways.

She said, 'I suppose we'd better ring him and make sure he hasn't forgotten the wedding.'

'He could hardly do that, surely,' I said.

'I wouldn't put it past him,' said Monica.

80

'Cynthia wouldn't let him,' said Margaret.

'What do you mean – Cynthia wouldn't let him?' said Monica in a tone of more positive contempt. 'Cynthia. Huh.'

Margaret did seem to have the knack of saying things designed to enrage her mother. I wondered if she did it deliberately. If so she was more interesting than I'd suspected. She could also be more trouble. I would prefer to be the only one to tease Monica. I didn't want her *too* disgruntled for she might get fed up with us. Couldn't have that. Margaret seemed to have gone off into a trance again so I spoke gently to Monica about the inadvisability of second marriages and how they so seldom worked. I didn't know if that was true or not, but it easily could be. Now I come to think of it, I think it probably is.

*

The evening dragged on. I remembered that I had bought a bottle of gin. I'd thought of keeping it in my room but it would be more useful to produce it now and make Monica tiddly. She was less disapproving when she was tiddly, and like most people she drank more when she wasn't drinking gin she had paid for herself. For some mysterious reason of her own Monica dragged in the subject of Syl's father. I had little to contribute to it, as you can imagine.

'He died of drink,' said Monica lugubriously. 'Drank himself to death.'

'Syl's late,' she added.

I was looking at Margaret as she spoke and Margaret, I can tell you, did not look like a girl waiting, all dewy-eyed, for her beloved. Not a bit. It made me uneasy. I didn't like sleeping with men nobody else wanted. There was no fun in it. I hope you're not shocked that I had resumed my fling with Syl. Why not? Why shouldn't I. Didn't do anybody any harm. Didn't even give me any pleasure. Even less now. It seemed depressingly pointless. Robert wouldn't be jealous if he knew. He'd only be – well, *disgusted* I think is the word. That was why he must never find out. He might have been jealous if I'd slept with the King of England but he'd be contemptuous if he knew I'd slept with Syl. I felt worse and worse as I realised increasingly that Margaret couldn't stand him either. You see my problem. A thief who gets away with the Crown Jewels is a bad person but a successful thief, while a thief who steals a bag of old sandwiches and apple cores from a person who already doesn't want them is a bad person and a bad thief and looks a perfect idiot in the eyes of everybody. Aargh. Nobody must ever know. They would lose all respect for me. I was in a hopeless position all round, and I was worried that Syl might have told his mother. She would despise me for different reasons – not because I had slept with her dear son who was a bit of a twerp, but because I had slept with her dear son without loving him any more. And I had an awful feeling that she had no proper reasons for despising me for sleeping with her husband – not gratifying reasons like jealousy and possessiveness and injured love. She had felt, I faintly realised, that anyone who fell for her husband's line was a bloody fool. That was probably why she seemed – oh God – *sorry* for me. It was pity that made her pleased to see me when I called. She thought I was so inadequate I must seek reassurance in the beds of old men, of other people's fiancés, of anyone who happened to be passing. It wasn't true. It's just that I have this reckless streak. I didn't want Syl's mother to despise me. I'd have to make a great effort to prove to her that I was strong and brave and attractive. Not lost and weak. I had an idea that by sleeping with all her menfolk I might have been trying to get closer to *her* – to gain some of her strength, to *identify* with her. I don't like thinking like this. It takes me too deep and I haven't got time to go down deep. And I never like what I find down there. Often I had thought that the women in the zenana might have been a comfort to each other – like Mother Joseph and her nuns. Well, not quite like that of course, but the ones who hated the sultan must have had a lot in common. When they were not mad with jealousy they must have been kind to each other.

I would go and see her again and make her laugh, and she would know that I was careless, and in control, and even if she found me shallow she would think me bright, and not be sorry for me at

83

all. I put aside the thought that she simply might not care.

*

Robert and Syl came in together. Oh hell. Where had they been? What had they been saying? Was *anything* worth all this worry? What was wrong with me that I danced around on the edge of trouble when there was no need for it? I think they'd just met on the doorstep. I hoped they'd just met on the doorstep. I was very vivacious that evening but my eyes didn't meet Syl's once. Abishag the Shulamite went off to bed. Robert went to bed. Syl went home. That left me and Monica and the rest of the gin. I do have a tendency to selfishness. Most people do, but I admit it – freely. I'd been thinking only of myself for days. I asked Monica how she was feeling and she began to tell me. She did look tired and I gave her a lot of gin. That as usual took us back into the past. After a few more gins she came up with a piece of the past I would really have preferred to have stayed buried in the mud at the bottom of the pool. I knew she hated Derek but I hadn't understood how much. Talking of the past I talked of him for he had been part of it. Not much of it, but he'd been there. Monica grew drunker and more hating. At her drunkest and hatefullest she told me Derek had molested his daughter when she was a little girl.

That silenced me, I can tell you. I couldn't think

84

of a word to say. To be honest, what I mostly felt at first was – thank God I never slept with Derek. Thank *God* I never slept with a child molester. If I had I cannot imagine what it would have done to my self-respect. I am glad to be able to say truthfully that my next feeling was one of pity. Real pity for Monica and Margaret. I am not a very good woman and I am not fond of children, but I know what every human being knows in the depths of his soul – that to hurt a child is a crime for which there is no forgiveness. I don't know about God but I do know that no human being can forgive an injury done to her child. Why should she? I didn't have a child. I didn't want one, but if I had I wouldn't. I have an unforgiving nature already and if someone had injured a child I had budded – oh, how I would have killed him. I gave Monica the rest of the gin and topped it up with vermouth and I had a lot myself and I don't really remember much of what we said after that. I think I may then have made her have a whisky and soda as a night-cap, for I knew it would be better by far if she forgot what she had told me.

*

I woke up early the next day remembering everything about the night before with complete clarity. My mind does this to me sometimes. I forget things I should remember and *vice versa*. I still felt drunk but clear-minded. Monica and Margaret slept late. Margaret always did but it was most unusual for Monica. I prayed that amnesia had overtaken her in the night. I was in the state where you can't make decisions – not even whether it's worth the effort of making yourself a piece of toast or putting the kettle on. At times like this I find it's easiest to go out. I went to see Syl's mother. What I really needed was another drink and I didn't want Monica to catch me at the Scotch bottle first thing in the morning. If by some fortunate chance she had forgotten her revelations of the night before it would be folly to jog her memory by letting her see how desperately in need of a drink the evening had left me the morning after. If you follow me.

Syl's mother offered me coffee and I felt I knew her well enough to turn it down and ask for whisky. There aren't all that many people you can do that to, so it was some indication of her worth.

And then, after a while and without too much preamble, I told her what Monica had told me. Now this time I *really* don't know why I did so. I had had no intention of telling her. None whatsoever. Could I have told her because I wanted her to know that there were worse people than me? Worse people who did much, much worse things than I did. Things that made my peccadillos seem almost like virtues. I hope it wasn't only that. I think it was more that I was still drunk and the sluice gates were open. How careful one should be, and how careful one is not when alcohol has eaten into the brain. I had another drink and a cigarette.

Syl's mother was naturally shocked. Well, she was more than shocked. I shouldn't have told her. It was indiscreet. It was more than indiscreet – it was unkind. On the other hand Monica shouldn't have told *me*. Why should I have to go round with that secret like a cockroach in my head? I *had* to tell someone and I was determined not to tell Syl. If Monica found out I'd told Syl the fat would, as they say, be in the fire. There would be the most frightful fuss. I might even find myself repudiated. You can see what the drink does to you. It suddenly occurred to me – and it felt like a kick in the stomach – that it was pretty damn silly to tell Syl's mother if I didn't want Syl to know. You'd think I might've thought of that before opening my mouth. But then, I thought, she wouldn't tell him because she was too old and too English and too strong. It may have been wishful thinking but it's what I thought. I trusted her. I thought she was strong enough to share another secret with me. Sometimes you love the people you share secrets with, and sometimes you hate them. A lot depends on the secret. Partners in crime can't be very fond of each other, but the recipient of the knowledge of another's frailty is in a rather good position; while the frail one is able to trust because if she's got any sense she knows that she has bowed her head to a superior person who will not dislike or reject her for doing so. It is similar to the dependency of the child on the mother; is it not? Oh well, maybe not.

87

All I'm saying is I didn't really repent of confiding in Mrs Monro – even if I should have done, and if you think I should, I don't agree with you.

*

The night of the exhibition came rather too soon. Although it was the reason we were in London it somehow caught me unprepared. Too many other things had happened and my mind was taken up with them. Robert was being a little too polite – not just to me. To everyone. It was unnatural. I was always polite when I'd done something I perhaps should not have done. For a while when I'd been a little careless I behaved very beautifully and made sure that everyone had just the amount of sugar he preferred in his coffee. I tiptoed a bit and smiled a lot and tried hard not to seem overbearing. It was obviously a mistake since it was such a give-away. I couldn't help it. I kept on deferring to Robert and Robert kept on being polite to me. *Why?* Do you know who Lilith was? She was Adam's first wife. And do you know why she left him? It was because she was sick and tired of lying underneath and she couldn't see why she should. She said 'Adam, I'm not going to lie underneath you any more. I'm going to be on top.' Adam argued about it because he had developed a liking for being on top and he wasn't prepared to abandon this position of dominance. They quarrelled and fought about it

88

for a long while between time and eternity, and neither would give way until Lilith got into such a rage that she left him. She grew vast black wings and soared above him and away to go and live in the deserts of the earth and brood about what a jerk he was. And Adam married Eve. I was right. Have *you* ever noticed how, when men marry for a second time, they usually choose a perfect drip? Some dumb, obedient female with the brains of a donkey? So she ruined everything by being such a dope and here we all are. Second wives are still the same. They're a push-over for door-to-door salesmen and when their husbands come home they say, 'Oh, darling, such a charming serpent called today and he sold me this apple. *Such* a bargain.' A husband with any sense would have made her ring up the parent company and demand her money back. He would if his first wife had done it, but not his second. No. All his confidence has gone and he doesn't want to upset the little woman in case she too might grow big black wings and leave him with his dinner spoiled in the oven.

Lilith grew very bitter when she saw how things were going. She despised Eve when she was pregnant and fat and she couldn't stand the children when they were small. She is still dangerous to pregnant women and children. I don't really blame her. I would not, myself, push over a pregnant woman in the street or drop poison dust in the babies' cradles, but I can see her point. Having made her stand it was all to no avail because stupid, wet Eve had come along and ruined it all. 'Yes, Adam. No, Adam. Ooh, that's lovely, Adam. Do it again.' I sometimes feel very defeated when I remember that Eve is the mother of us all. What hope have we? What hope when we spring from bossy, old Adam and limp, silly Eve? Syl's mother, I felt, was cast more in the mould of Lilith. Perhaps that was why I liked her. She was like me.

I have been avoiding the subject of the exhibition because of what happened. What happened was this. We all went along in our best frocks. Monica and Margaret and Syl and his mother and Robert and me. And I was going to behave perfectly with *politesse* and charm and sobriety. Behave as only I can behave when I put my mind to it. It was Margaret who opened my eyes. Limp, silly Margaret. Can you believe it? She was drifting up and down, looking at the pictures, and she suddenly opened her mouth and said: 'That's Marie Claire's gate.' I'd seen that picture before. Of course I had. I'd seen all the damn things dozens of times, but I'd never really *looked* at them. Not properly. She was right. It *was* Marie Claire's gate. Why hadn't I seen that before? Because I didn't want to, I suppose. I suppose I *had* seen it and not admitted it to myself. I suppose that was why I'd been feeling so anxious. For a moment I went blind and deaf and senseless. Oh God. I went into automatic. I said a lot of things off the top of my head. I was practised at that. Luckily Celestine was there so I talked to her. Talked and talked and talked. I began to feel better. I began to say to myself that a painting of a person's gateway meant nothing at all. He could have painted it at any time. He could have painted it from memory. I talked to Syl about something or other and had another drink and a fag and took a few deep breaths and moved down the gallery ...

I think they do it to English sheep. They don't just cut their throats. I think they stun them first and then come in with the *coup de grace*. That's what happened to me. I was beginning to recover from the shock when I came to a picture of a bedroom scene. Now the mad, the stupid thing about this is that I did remember that picture. I had been in the room when Robert was fiddling with it. I had said, 'What a *sluttish* woman with her clothes all over the floor.' I had assumed that he was painting not from memory, but from imagination. Silly Lili, eh? Would anybody have believed that Lili could be so blind? I began to plan what I should do to Marie Claire. A number of ideas occurred to me. Not all of them feasible. I looked at her back and thought how it would be improved by the addition of a great big hat pin. I thought of something to do to Robert too. He had come up beside me and put his hand on my shoulder. I wanted to take his hand and pull away his jacket from his shoulder and bite him in his upper arm until the blood ran, until my teeth met his bone. 'Oh,' I said, 'look at the crocodile pool. How the people shouted when you went too near it.'

'How do you know?' asked Robert, taking his hand away. 'You weren't there.' Did he know that I

91

knew? Had I said enough to let him know that I knew? Had I been sufficiently *dégagé* yet obviously aware? Had I managed to give the impression that I had *always* known? That I didn't really care?

'They kept finding bodies in it,' said Robert, and Margaret fainted.

I was quite relieved although I did think to myself — What's *she* got to faint about? If anyone should be lying on the floor of the gallery it should be me. Still, it stopped me having to say anything more. I was faintly worried that I was going to lose my temper and hit my husband until he died, there in the crowded gallery, and then everyone would have known how much I minded that he had been unfaithful to me with Marie Claire. With *Marie Claire*, who was even sillier than Eve. Oh, it was insupportable.

People were fussing round Margaret. She was hanging on to me and Monica was demanding to know what she thought she was doing. Syl said he'd take her home and looked at me over the top of her head. I looked back at him, but all I said was, 'How kind.' I didn't need to say any more.

Robert said, 'Well, the evening seems to be over. We'd better get to the restaurant. Coming, Lili?' And I said, 'Robert, I'd rather stick needles in my eyes.'

*

I took a taxi all the way back and I smoked and
smoked cigarette after cigarette. When I got to
Monica's house I went round into the garden. It
was dark but the distant street lights meant I could
just see my way. I went straight to the summer-
house where Syl was waiting for me.

*

Syl liked to talk afterwards. He always had and it's
surprising how people don't change. It was
freezing cold and uncomfortable in that damned
summer-house. Well, you can imagine. But I was
still so angry I felt hot. I had taken charge over the
last half hour. My aunts had had a book which was
always given to the residents of the Zenana when
the Sultan gave the word. A manual of technique.
It was wasted on Syl who seemed to take it all for
granted. I had never used these esoteric skills with
Robert because I thought I loved him enough not
to need to. Maybe I should have done. Oh well.
What the hell. And if you are thinking these are
prostitutes' skills you are wrong. These are the
skills of the concubine. Yes, there *is* a difference,
but I haven't got time to argue about it.

'What were you saying, Syl?' I asked. 'Sorry. I
wasn't listening.'

He didn't mind my saying this polite and
unloverly thing. I was wrapped in a ghastly old
blanket, smoking a cigarette and wondering what I

could do next to annoy Robert. I was saving up Marie Claire to think about when I had a lot of time and no distractions.

I stretched out my elbow and knocked over a flower pot. Damn. It had Monica's cactus in it. She kept the nasty thing as a pet. It was a winter-flowering thing and she talked about it a lot. Boasted about it. 'Greenfingers', she said. I had to put the light on to pick it up. It was a little bit broken, but I turned it round and it looked all right. I could see Syl now the light was on so I turned it off again.

'I should really have married you, Lili,' said Syl. 'We're the same sort of people.'

If I hadn't been so upset already this would have led me to utter a few words. It was just as well I couldn't think of anything to say. I was no more like Syl than I was like the kitchen sink. How extra-ordinary men are – I thought. I was beginning to feel tired. Married to Syl? Me? I'd rather be married to the kitchen sink. I was also beginning to feel a little disgusted with myself.

'Get your clothes on, Syl,' I said.

'I'm not cold,' he said.

I didn't give a toot whether he was cold or not. I just wanted him to put his clothes on. I put mine on, stumbling about in the dark and getting things back to front. How interesting it would be if I should go to the house with my dress inside out and cigarette ends in my hair and everyone was there, sitting in the drawing-room, sipping coffee and eating bis-cuits. 'Good evening, Lili. What *have* you been doing?' 'Me? Oh, I've just been ...'

94

'What's the time, Syl?' I said.

'It's not late,' he said, sliding his hand down my leg. Oh God, now he was going to be affectionate. What a fool you are sometimes, Lili. It *was* late. It was a bit too late to tell him to keep his hands to himself.

'Tell me about Abishag the ... tell me about Margaret,' I said.

He took his hand off my leg and put it on the back of my neck. I suppose he thought that was a more respectable place if we were going to discuss his forthcoming marriage. He'd always been peculiar about women. He fell in love the way people, who are run-down, catch colds. Yes, I do it too, but not *all* the time. *He* was prone to it and he did it all the time. Here a thought struck me. What – since Syl had such appalling taste in women – did he see in me? I reminded myself that I was calling the shots here. I had instigated this meeting. It was quite possible that he saw nothing in me at all. I had never thought I should find comfort in picturing myself as undesirable. You see, the twists that you can take once you get off the beaten track. Syl was much too stupid to see the flame in me. I was inviolate. Oh, Lilith.

'You see, Lili,' he said, 'she has these banked-down fires in her ...' I was amazed at my percipience. There I was thinking about fires and there was Syl talking about them. 'She's been kept down by her mother all her life,' he went on. 'She has a warm nature and she's capable of passion, but it's all been diverted into other channels. Into

95

mother love ...' I thought if Margaret loved her mother I was the cat's granny, but I didn't say anything. 'In her,' he said, 'it's as if the river was running backwards towards the source. She's got this sense of duty towards her mother because her father abandoned her and that makes it difficult for her to show emotion. But it's *there*,' he said with conviction.

I thought – oh nuts, Syl – but I only said '*What* her?'

'What?' said Syl.

'What *her*?' I asked. 'You speak of too many hers. There's the her who's running backwards, and the her who was abandoned and the her who can't show emotion. *What* her?'

'You know perfectly well,' said Syl. He'd always been given to this sort of thing. He'd tried it on me once. It was a kind of guard against rejection. As yet another female turned him down he'd worry at the matter like a rat in a dry well until he'd rationalised his loss and restored his *amour-propre*. I had once said to him 'Oh, do put all that away, Syl' – or something on those lines – and he'd said my reason for saying it was that my mother had neglected me. The reason I'd said it was that I was waiting for somebody else to come and spend the night, and the reason he was coming to spend the night wasn't because my mother had neglected me, I can tell you. Try explaining that to Syl.

I was sick of Syl. I'd had a sudden nasty feeling that perhaps we *were* the same sort of people, or, at least, not totally unalike. What a dreadful thought.

I had used him. I hated him. The time had come to pull the plug and run. But I *had* been on top.

*

Next day was bad. Really bad. Monica was wild with Margaret for passing out, Robert was wild with me for not going to dinner with them, I was wild with Robert, and Syl was wild because his honeymoon was cancelled. The charlady was wild too. She was trying to do the cleaning and listen to us talking at the same time. Not as easy as you might think. You can only polish one bit of floor for five minutes or so, then you have to move on out of earshot. 'Oh,' I had said, being as spiteful as I knew how and speaking as a *Masri*. 'You *can't* take the little one to Egypt at this time of year if she isn't well. She'd catch all manner of things.' Why should Syl go to Egypt. Darling Egypt was too good for him. I really hated him today. I kept remembering parts of the night before and going 'Ouch' and 'Oh God' and closing my eyes and clutching my hair and wishing I'd died. I had to pretend I had a migraine. How *could* I have.... No, never mind. Let's think about something else.

Margaret said, 'I hope I didn't spoil the evening.'

And Robert said, '*You* didn't spoil the evening.' He looked at me and then away. What was I supposed to do when my husband painted pictures of his mistress and hung them around for everyone to see? Call them all to come and watch? 'Now this is Marie Claire. She's just crawled out of bed and my husband thought that would be a good time to do a nice painting of her.' How I wanted to kill him. I was very calm and controlled and I said the exhibition had been a conspicuous success and wasn't that heartening; and I said I'd been tired and come home and gone to bed early, and I looked straight at Robert and dared him to call me a liar and he just *yawned*.

Monica said they'd been looking for me for hours, and I thought that in a way it was a pity they hadn't looked in the summer-house.

'Sorry,' I said.

What if they had looked through the window at the moment when ...? No, it wasn't funny. I was going to laugh. I turned it into a hiccup and said, 'Sorry,' again. I *was* sorry. I was sorry I'd degraded my person with Syl, but, yes, in some wicked way it was terribly, terribly funny.

*

'I want to talk to you, Lili,' said Robert. Oh God. We were in our bedroom chastely clad in pyjamas and night-gown. He stood at one side of the bed, poised to get in, and I stood at the other waiting for him to do so. I was carefully behaving like a married lady rather than a *houri*.

'Yes dear?' I said. That was going too far. I never

called him 'dear' just like that. He looked at me without smiling. 'Whatsa matter?' I asked. That was the wrong thing to say too. Why should anything be the matter? I began to work myself into a rage. If anything was the matter it was his infidelity. His unforgivable infidelity. Bastard.

But he wanted to talk about money. Robert worried much more about money than he did about human relationships. In this he was quite different from me. All right, in a way I did expect money to grow on trees. In a way, for me, it did. It was the fault of my aunts. They had the minds of merchants. To the merchant there is always something to buy and sell, and even if you don't make a profit the money goes round and round. I did not have the mentality of a merchant. I had the mentality of a child of merchants. That is, I thought money grew on trees. Robert, needlessly, reminded me of this and he intended his remarks as a reproach. I could not see why an ability to account and save should be considered a moral attribute; and I could see nothing wrong in spending money when you had it. Just as long as you always had something to sell should the need arise. He said we were not too badly off at the moment for, while his pictures did not yet command a great price, the exhibition should prove to be a financial success. He said the money he had made in the deal over his grandpapa's things was a help, but he also said that we had to pay off our debts, and to this end he had borrowed a little money from Syl in order to enable us to

99

travel to Scotland without touching the money in the bank.

What? He'd borrowed money from Syl? When? What did they talk about while he was doing this borrowing? And what was that story – the one about the man who wanted to sleep with the merchant's wife? She said it would cost him, so he borrowed the money from the merchant, had his fun, and when the merchant asked for the money back he said he'd already given it to his wife. Why did I think of that story? It was the other way round wasn't it? My mind was fuddled but I was relieved Robert was only talking about money. As for human relationships I'd decided to call it quits for the time being. I knew that no matter what he'd done, when the chips were down I'd be the one to get the blame. *All* the blame. I would just wait, and one of these days ... I made a vow. And I *always* kept my word.

'Why are we going to Scotland, Robert?' I asked, climbing into bed sideways with my knees together and smelling of toothpaste and talcum.

'You don't have to come,' he said. Maybe I didn't, but I was. I was going to stay very close to Robert for a while. We'd been playing a dangerous game. Time to stick together until the boat stopped rocking. I didn't want either of us straying anywhere; not alone. It appeared there was a gallery in Edinburgh which had expressed interest in his work and he was going to discuss the possibility of another exhibition. I vowed that, in future, I too would take a greater interest in his

100

work. I'd follow him round and hold his brushes.

*

Scotland was cold.

*

I had bought whisky and biscuits as presents and a large, warm red coat for Lili. A very expensive, large red coat. It suits me. 'Robert,' I had said, 'I don't care what you say, I'm not going to freeze to death for want of a warm red coat. You can sell an extra picture.'

Margaret was pleased when we came back. She must have missed me. She wanted to talk and I felt sorry for her. It must have been so boring when we went away and she was left on her own with Monica. She had a funny idea of social chit-chat, mind you. She was always talking about age and death. Well, not always, because she didn't talk all that much, but when she did she usually talked about age and death. I hope she didn't do it because she thought I was the expert. I also had a tendency to talk about age and death when I felt tired. I do us both an injustice. Margaret knew I wasn't as silly as I seemed to some people.

'You mustn't worry about age,' I said. 'It doesn't

matter.' Oh, listen to me. Listen to Lili, whistling in the dark. Would Robert love me when my teeth fell out? What if my hair fell out? Would children have kept us together for ever? No, of course not. It was people without children who stayed together for ever. I told her to keep up appearances. Loads of make-up. Expensive clothes. Avoid the elderly. Stick with the young. Oh Lord, what an awful thought – tottering round on your poor swollen old feet, keeping up with the hopelessly, madly boring *young*.

The young are so moral and principled and full of high ideals. I hate them. I didn't say that. You'd be surprised if you knew how sensible I can sound when I talk. You should ask Margaret. I gave her a lot of good advice. I said a number of wise and sensible things. We had an excellent conversation until Monica butted in and that was the end of that. Monica was not only incapable of conversation – she made everyone else start sounding like mother's little idiot child. It was infuriating. Down went the tone of my elevated conversation.

It went down so far that Robert put in his pennyworth and accused me of talking tripe. That did it. I had been as good as gold in Scotland. I had been as good as gold for several days. I had talked about bloody old art and sat with my ankles crossed and crooked my little finger when drinking tea. *Tea*. I hadn't even made any crumbs. Everyone we'd met had fallen in love with me and I'd been gracious to them. No more. Just gracious. And what thanks did I get? I got told I talked tripe. OK,

Robert, that was enough of little goody-two-shoes. I wondered where I should go that night. I'd think of somewhere – and I'd think of someone to be there with me. Nobody important, nobody dangerous – just somebody Robert wouldn't approve of. I'd probably settle for Celestine in the end. We could go dancing. I was knitting together this small and none too sinister plot when Monica made one of her daft remarks.

'I'm sure Cynthia will never get the children's clothes right,' she said. Don't ask me why she said it then. Her mind worked that way. It sort of got in and out of the water like a frog on a lily pad and you never knew what it was going to do next.

'Let us go and see,' I said. 'Let us go to Cynthia's house and have a look.' And in case you're wondering I don't know why I said that. Partly boredom, partly curiosity, I suppose. I rather enjoy observing strange creatures in their natural habitat and it would be interesting to see how Monica carried herself. 'Go and ring her,' I said. 'See what she says.'

Monica was very funny on the phone. Not intentionally of course. No, she was polite and condescending. I was surprised she'd agreed so quickly. Perhaps she was curious about Derek's new home too, and nobody had ever been sufficiently considerate to give her the chance of visiting it. She was probably grateful to me.

'We'll go down on Thursday,' she said, 'and have lunch there.'

Came a point when I had to get out of the house again or murder Monica. She wouldn't stop talking about clothes and weddings. I wouldn't have minded if she'd had *anything* interesting to say, but she hadn't. Not a thing. White satin, smoked salmon – oh Yuk. Besides, getting married meant you had to live together and at the moment I thought living together was a lousy idea. For better for worse – and worse. If it had been accepted that we should live apart then Robert, when we met, would have no idea that I'd been up to anything. He would love pure Lili, the angel. On the other hand, I would have no idea what Robert had been up to. This could be a good thing since it would mean less anxiety for me – in a way. I would, perhaps, always be suspicious, and that is so exhausting. Oh, it was *all* too exhausting. All this running around. It made me think of Syl when I didn't really want to. Syl ran around like a puppy dog; like the worst sort of puppy dog you can't take out without trouble. At the sight of a female he'd dash off, tail wagging. *Any* female would get him running around going 'Bark, bark' and scrabbling with his little paws for attention. You'd call 'To heel' and there he'd be dancing round, twirling his moustaches. What I mean is – if he hadn't been a dog he'd have been a moustache-twirler, a Ladies' Man. Oh God. He'd been doing it at the exhibition until Margaret fell over. I was getting madder with Robert by the minute for forcing me into the arms of Syl. Oh, *damn* and blast. *I* didn't scrabble with my paws for attention.

*

I went to see Mrs Monro. She was refreshing. I couldn't imagine how she'd managed to be the wife and mother of those two men. Not that it's all that unusual. I have known several rather magnificent women with the *most* hopeless husbands and sons. I suppose they seem even more hopeless beside their magnificent woman. I wondered how people saw me and Robert.

I took a box of biccies someone had given me in Scotland round to Mrs Monro as a present, and she was *pleased to see me*. She was. She was really pleased. I can tell. Oh, it is so warming when someone is really pleased to see you. I could talk to her. Not about Robert any more because every time I thought of Robert being so annoying I thought of vengeance and I couldn't tell her that, so I didn't talk about Robert. I sat down and said Monica and I were going to see Cynthia and Derek to make sure they'd put buttons on the kiddies' frocks.

'Eugh,' said Mrs Monro, 'Derek. I don't think I'll be able to look at him. I can't think how Monica can bear to look at him.'

But I knew that even if they remembered what

had happened they wouldn't really remember, neither Monica nor Derek. I knew how bad people lived with themselves. After a while they pretended somebody else had done it – no matter what it was. Even now I was beginning to pretend that some other person had spent the better part of a night in a moth-eaten old summer-house. Not me. Not Lili. No.

Mrs Monro wished Derek was dead. I told her that bad people always started to die before they died, that corruption was a sign of death. Dear Lord. But I wasn't bad, not really stinkingly bad, not so bad the angels would have to hold their noses. Was I? I was so glad Syl's mother didn't know the last bad thing I'd done.

*

Eve, as well as being a gullible mug, was a dreadful housewife. Cynthia was a dreadful housewife and she clearly couldn't cope with little Cain and Abel – or rather little Jennifer and Christopher. Their beastly, depressing small toys lay around everywhere, broken. There was mud in the garden and the children smelt. Cynthia was skinny and hairy and gummy. Much worse than Monica. Derek had married Eve twice, but Eve II was far worse than Eve I. Monica was dumb in many ways but she was moderately competent in the house, and she washed. Cynthia looked as though a good wash

106

wouldn't do her any harm. It was Monica who said this. She whispered it to me when Cynthia wasn't listening. Mind you, she couldn't have been *sure* Cynthia wasn't listening since she'd only that second gone out of the door. Oh, I had to make such an effort to handle the children's little frocks. Both the little children had necks like the necks of dead chickens – dirty dead chickens. Everything here was thin and dirty. How I began to appreciate Monica and her house. How I hated Cynthia's food. I didn't eat it. I sat there hating it and pushing it round the plate. The plate was greasy with old grease. The house was cold with a scum of greasy dust. It was like hell. Derek had married again and gone to hell. Good. I wondered if he abused his new little children and what progression of hells he would go through until he himself crumbled away into greasy dust. I thought that never, never again would I do an impure thing, for I must be different from Derek and free of all that dirt and dust. Once I had believed that transgression led to freedom but now I looked and I saw where it led. Oh no, the place wasn't *really* as bad as that – not in actuality. It was bad enough but something else gave it its atmosphere. Derek, I suppose. I could never be as bad as Derek if I lived forever, but I wasn't good enough to be comfortable. Oh damn.

Cynthia had put Peter Pan collars on the children's frocks so I took them off again. I didn't bother much with their clothes for there wasn't any point. They would look like dressed-up dead

107

chickens whatever I did. Cynthia gave them pickled red things for their lunch – cabbage and beetroot with bitter, dripping juices designed to ruin blue velvet. I had to be so careful to keep them apart. I wanted to go out and buy a clean towel to sit on. I wanted to get away.

I said, 'Monica, we must go now, for we have things to do this evening.'

'Yes,' said Monica, who was quite good at this game. 'We don't want to keep everybody waiting.' We had given the impression that away from here, in glorious Croydon full of light, there were fascinating and numerous people looking at their watches and wondering eagerly where we were. Cynthia looked wistful.

'Oh Monica,' I said, as we closed the garden gate on the mud and the broken toys.

'I suppose she does her best,' said Monica in a tone of contentment.

I was so glad to be back in Croydon. I know that must sound strange but it's true. I am a little afraid of poverty in all its forms – actual and spiritual. I wonder sometimes what would become of a person who had lost everything; how she would even begin to think about how to begin again if she had nothing at all to sell and nothing to offer freely. It didn't bear thinking about. Monica, admittedly, did not go in for oriental luxury, but her house was a dream of cleanliness and comfort compared with Cynthia's. It didn't frighten me. I could not have stayed a moment longer in Cynthia's house without bursting into tears of fear and depression. This would have been most unlike me. Perhaps I was catching a cold. Perhaps I was growing old. Well, I wasn't a mess. Cynthia was a mess. Her house was a mess, her children were messes, her husband was worse than any mess. Her clothes were almost worse than anything. I was tired. I had to have a drink. Monica had a drink too, but for the other reason. There are two reasons for drinking as far as I'm concerned – because you're happy or because you're sad. Monica was happy now she knew that Derek lived in the dust.

'I want a drink too,' said Margaret. It was really too early for all this drinking, but – so what. I went to the cloakroom in the hall and nearly fell over the cleaning lady's bucket. She had a most disconcerting way of appearing out of nowhere. She had her hat on, so was on her way home. 'Careful,' she said. And then she said, 'You want to watch that husband of yours.' She was looking towards the drawing-room door as she spoke – looking at Margaret slumped in an armchair. She couldn't have said that, could she? I knew she rather liked me. I had seen her grinning to herself at things I had said while she mopped and dusted, but we had never actually spoken directly to each other. Why should we? Why should she now say such a thing to me? For my sake or for the sake of Margaret? Was that *really* what she had said? I couldn't ask her. I had already smiled at her and moved back to the drawing-room. When she opened her mouth to speak I had assumed that she would say 'Good-evening-lovely-weather-for-the-time-of-year' and it was to that expected remark that

109

I had responded – not 'You should keep your eye on your husband' or whatever it was she'd said. I couldn't think how I should respond to such a remark from the cleaning lady. Did she mean to imply that Robert had spent the day pursuing Abishag the Shulamite round the house? I really couldn't quite visualise this happening. For one thing it seemed to me that Margaret wouldn't run. She would sit there gazing in incomprehension at any male who showed signs of getting up speed in her direction. So, naturally, he would wind down again and pretend that he had merely been trying to take a moth out of her ear. Maybe that's what had happened. Oh hell, what did I care. I did care. Nobody in the world, as long as I lived and all through eternity should ever know how much I minded about Robert. Certainly not Robert. Certainly not Marie Claire, the cow.

I said 'Did Marie Claire explain why she wouldn't come to the wedding?' Monica had been partly aggrieved at this refusal and partly relieved for she didn't want her house overwhelmed with people. You can't keep a house tidy when it's full of people. I thought – she daren't come in case I know about her and Robert. She's frightened I'll kill her. Quite a lot of killing went on where we lived. Well, not a *lot*, but it tended to be more casual than English killing. People tended to disappear sometimes, or they got ill and died. Sometimes their families minded a great deal and sometimes they didn't. I wouldn't have killed Marie Claire. I wouldn't have given her the satisfaction. Monica said Marie Claire

110

was too busy, and then Margaret suddenly said, 'I don't want to marry Syl.' Of course she didn't. Nobody ever had – not for long anyway. For a second I felt sorry for Syl. He wasn't all that bad. Not really. There was just something a bit wrong with him. Something a bit weird. He wasn't a eunuch. No. But there was something smooth about him, something incomplete. He wasn't really a proper human being, let alone a proper man. Oh, poor Syl. Then I looked at Margaret. Looked at her properly for the first time for days. Ever. And I thought poor Margaret, and then I thought – poor me, and after a while I even thought – poor Robert. It must have been the gin. No. It wasn't altogether the gin for I am not incapable of human sympathy. I only wish I was. This wouldn't do. Lili was going soft.

*

I'd made Syl buy one of Robert's paintings. Syl didn't like parting with money. I'd told him it would make a superb wedding present for the bride, and I wouldn't let him off the hook. 'You buy that picture,' I said, 'and I tell you what I'll do. I'll take you out to dinner in a little French restaurant I know.' Syl couldn't resist that – a free meal *and* with Lili. 'Besides,' I told him, 'that picture is a bargain. You can make such a profit on it one day.' It was getting very close to the time for

111

this assignation and I suddenly rather lost my head. 'Let us,' I said, 'go and have dinner in Soho. It will make a nice change for Margaret.' As I spoke I thought to myself – Lili, you've gone mad. What are you doing? What do you think you're doing? I knew what I was doing. I was dicing with death. The reckless streak had overwhelmed me. Sometimes I had swum in crocodile-infested waters. Once I had overturned a stall in the *souk*. Oh yes, I had. I had been a good girl for days and when I saw the peasants quietly buying mangoes I had seized a support under the stall and pulled it away. There was nothing anyone could do about it. Not to me. The mangoes had rolled everywhere, and after that I had been good again for weeks.

I changed my mind. I thought I would take them to another restaurant, but Monica said, 'What about Robert? What will Robert do about dinner?' and I remembered the picture of Marie Claire in her dreadful bedroom, and I thought of how *smug* Monica could be, and I thought – oh, so what the hell. What the flaming hell. And I drove to the restaurant of the assignation with Syl. I sang as I drove.

*

It all fell flat. We sat there in the little restaurant discussing the menu over one of those nasty candlesticks, dripping with wax, and nothing

112

happened. Syl stuck his head round the door but when he saw three of us he bolted like a rabbit. Men are such cowards. Stupid too, I'd been going to smile at him *so* sweetly, and tell him I'd arranged all this as a little extra celebration. If he'd kept his head he could have carried it off but guilt had lent wings to his heels. I did smile as I thought of him flying down the street clutching Robert's picture, his heart pounding; head in a whirl – all confused. 'What is Lili up to?' he would be asking himself. 'What's her game?' Let him stew. I choked on a mouthful of *moules marinières* as something occurred to me. Speaking literally, Syl would be allowed to keep his head, unlike the male relations of the lover of the silly Sultana.

Monica said, 'I could have sworn that was Syl – he opened the door and looked straight at me and went straight out again.'

'Perhaps it was him,' I said. 'He works somewhere round here, doesn't he?'

'Can't have been,' said Monica. 'Why would he go like that? What are you laughing at?' I caught Margaret looking at me and I had the feeling that she knew what I'd been doing. Knew about the assignation and everything. Didn't care. Somewhere inside me I worried about Margaret. She was not fit to take part in these games. She was not like the rest of us. Don't get the wrong idea. I didn't think she was too *good* for the game – not better than the rest of us – only not *designed* for the game. And I felt that if I was going to bring her into the game then I should have to wash my hands. Yes –

here it came, that annoying feeling that one must not sully innocence. Even the knowledge that one is capable of sullying innocence is annoying. It makes one feel corrupt – and old.

I sang all the way home too – out of spite.

*

Damn. I did feel corrupt. It was all Margaret's fault. Little milky mouse with sad eyes. She looked at me so mournfully sometimes with those eyes, as though she wanted me to save her. To march in and pick her up and send her back to Mother Joseph and the clear fountain. How could I? How was I to explain to Monica the nature of vocation? I wasn't too sure about it myself – it was nothing I'd ever experienced. If Mother Joseph wanted her, let her come and get her. Nothing to do with me. I wasn't her mother. I rather needed a mother myself. I went to see Syl's one. I ran there.

Mrs Monro was unsentimental and strong-minded. I couldn't think how she'd ever conceived Syl, who was neither. But I couldn't discuss Syl with her. I told her about the trip to Cynthia's house. I told her how awful Cynthia was, and her food. I didn't really want to talk about Cynthia. I wanted to tell her how destructive I could be and ask her why she thought that was. I wanted to confess. I couldn't, of course, for that would have brought in Syl – not to mention his father. I approached it

114

from another way. I was beginning to feel rather proud of the depth of my concern for Margaret. I wasn't used to worrying about people other than Robert or myself and I felt if I really worried about Margaret I should not only seem, but *be*, a better person.

I heard myself saying, 'We must think about Margaret.'

'And Syl,' said his mother. Oh bother Syl – I thought, but I didn't say it. She went on: 'Margaret is much too young for him. She's not ready for marriage.'

'I know,' I said. I couldn't for the life of me see what was to be done about it. There was no point in talking to Monica, for the whole thing was her idea. I was sure Margaret would never have let things go this far without her mother pushing and pushing.

'This wedding would be most unfortunate,' I said. 'A disaster.' Syl's mother agreed. She *was* a sensible woman. I didn't want to hurt her maternal feelings by remarking that anyone who married Syl would be letting herself in for disaster, so I explained that Margaret had a vocation and thus was in no position to marry anybody without incurring the wrath of God – the jealous God whom no one in her right mind would care to cross. Vocation, the religious life, wasn't something I really wanted to talk about much. I liked Mother Joseph. I was fond of Mother Joseph, but she always made me feel as though I'd do well to go and have a ritual bath and a good scrub – inside and out. I couldn't imagine living the life of a nun although I had to admit it would be peaceful with no men around. But, oh, so boring. I stopped thinking like that for if God knows all our thoughts he would not be flattered to hear me thinking that a life dedicated to his service would be boring. I really didn't feel I could afford to offend anyone at the moment – let alone God.

Syl's mother was interested in all I could tell her about the convent. She kept wanting to know more and I didn't know much more. I just wished I knew more about what Marie Claire had been up to, and I couldn't think of any way of finding out. I rather wished she *was* coming over for the wedding. It would have offered opportunities for revenge – my favourite condiment. But no. I had to stop thinking like that. It always led to trouble. Mostly trouble for other people, but quite often it splashed up on me.

I said, 'Marie Claire won't come to the wedding. She's frightened of me.' On the face of it this was a pointless remark. Something drove me to say: 'She doesn't know I know she's been having an affair with Robert.' I had to tell somebody. It was rankling in me. 'Good heavens,' said Syl's mother, not sounding too perturbed.

'But she's not sure I won't find out,' I said. I found it difficult to leave the subject alone, but for the moment Syl's mother was more interested in Margaret than in me. I began to try and think of something else. I looked round and tried to picture Margaret living here. It wasn't possible. It was too *sad*, too depressing. This house needed somebody with a bit of sparkle. Syl's mother needed

116

somebody with a bit of sparkle. Margaret would just fade like the curtains, go limp like the cushions and all the lights would get dimmer and dimmer. Poor Margaret.

'A nun,' said Mrs Monro reflectively, 'a nun. Yes, I see.'

'I believe it,' I said. 'There was some fuss in Egypt – some rubbish Marie Claire was going on about – but I think the nun part is all true.'

'I think so too,' said Mrs Monro. 'I really don't think there ought to be a wedding.'

'I don't think there will be,' I said, and I meant that I would stop it.

*

I don't know when I made up my mind that I must keep my word. It might have been just then when Mrs Monro looked at me as though she trusted me, as though she thought I might be capable of anything. Well, I *was* capable of anything. In the end I proved it. Or it might have been when the cleaning lady told me Robert was not to be trusted alone with Margaret. Or it might have been when Margaret had looked at me with big trusting eyes and almost asked me aloud to help her – to please, please help her. I don't know. I have a destructive impulse in me – often I have thought of suicide and sometimes of murder – but I don't know what I then had decided to destroy. Monica's hopes? Or

Syl's? Or Robert's? Or just me. Or perhaps I simply couldn't resist the compulsion to go centre stage; what Robert called 'showing off'. Oh, I was angry with Robert. Not only because of Marie Claire, but because often he had made me feel insecure. He had assumed superiority over me and I'd let him get away with it. The time of reckoning – I said to myself – had come. Fasten your seat-belts.

And all the time, of course, I told myself that I could change my mind when it came to the point. I was not committed to anything. I let Monica go on fussing – about the wedding and the wedding guests and the food and the wine and the clothes – and occasionally I felt a little mean for it was all to come to nothing, but mostly I let her go on as though I were in a dream. As though in one of those dreams where impossible things happen together, at the same time. I seemed to leave my body as a jinni leaves a bottle and float above all the people, invulnerable, omnipotent and – not to be trusted. Everybody knows that the jânn can't be trusted. They share with man the promise of salvation but they go round at night doing bad things. It wasn't my fault. I hadn't let myself out of the bottle, had I? Robert had uncorked the bottle with his infidelity; or maybe it was Margaret with her hopeless trust; or maybe it was Peri or Lilith and I had liberated myself on huge wings of rage. Also, to be honest, I foresaw some fun. I knew I should cause the most alarming scene but scenes can be such fun – especially years later when the dust has settled and the blood dried. It would come as a shock to Monica, but by then the exhibition would be all over and it wouldn't matter any more. Besides, Monica's sensibilities wouldn't be so refined if she hadn't been so stuck-up in the old days. I could have taken her to places to see all manner of things that would have done a good deal to broaden her mind. She'd always said she didn't care for that type of thing – said it with her nose in the air. Some of us had been unable to avoid that type of thing. Who did she think she was? A dancer has to dance in some strange places. Then sometimes I remembered her when she hadn't been so annoying. When she was a girl sometimes she was fun. And sometimes, every now and then, I remembered a tiny little thing in a little sashed frock and that was Margaret, and I would think that such a little one should never, never be invited to step into a dancing house in Cairo. I was not getting sentimental. It merely seemed unsuitable. Syl would not have seemed out of place in such an establishment. Especially not since ... oh, never mind.

We practised wearing our wedding clothes, and I adjusted Monica's collar under her chin and asked how the winter-flowering cactus was coming along, and I smiled into her eyes.

*

Oh God. Derek and Cynthia arrived with Cain and

Abel and their potty. No, I do not regret not having had any children. I hate the small creatures. They cried and whined in tiny voices like the voices of caterpillars. Oh, the poor little things. No, I won't be sorry for them. I won't. I couldn't afford pity. I hadn't got the time for it.

They arrived with a lot of depressing objects; a lot of their smaller broken toys, and I think they all had a bit of mud on their feet. Nobody could possibly be pleased to see them. Nobody was. They dropped things it was hard to see the purpose of. You couldn't imagine why they'd bothered to pack them. You couldn't imagine why they'd come at all.

Monica was haughty and Cynthia was abstracted and everybody else was embarrassed, so I kissed them all – except for Monica, naturally – and I lit a cigarette to take the taste away. I wished *I* was away. I wished I was lying in the sun, drunk somewhere, with somebody terribly, terribly witty and clever, trickling oil into the small of my back. I don't know why people cling so to life when it is so seldom pleasant. But perhaps I exaggerate. No one would want to live for long in the vicinity of Derek and Cynthia, but there were other forms of life around. I think I had been drinking too much again. If I went on it wouldn't be long before the horrors got me. I should have to get back to the sun. Who should I take with me? No, not Robert. Not yet. I didn't know if I could ever forgive him enough to let him rub oil in my back again. I reflected that I hadn't spent a sober night since I had arrived in England. Not good enough, Lili. There was no real cure for the horrors. You had to go on, trying to drink rather less, until they went away. But what if they never went away? Then you died, I suppose. Died in the dark, screaming at the black wings to go away, screaming for your mother and the monkey your father brought you. Screaming that you hadn't meant it, that you never meant to destroy anything – not even yourself. Oh *God*.

I said to Monica that I found Derek and Cynthia acutely lowering to the spirits, hoping she would also feel sufficiently down to suggest a drink. This was the right thing to say. We went into the drawing-room and after a while I felt better.

Cain and Abel had their supper in the kitchen and Eve put them to bed. She stayed up there with them and Derek also went up early. I didn't think about that. I had drunk enough by now to persuade myself that Monica had been lying about her ex-husband for I didn't want to spoil the whisky by gazing at the devil's feet. Derek made me think of the devil's feet. I was getting drunk again, and where was Robert? Abishag the Shulamite had also gone early to bed. At least I supposed she had. Yes, of course, she had. I wasn't drunk enough to imagine she was rolling round in the garden with my husband who had to have an eye kept on him. Nor in the summer-house.

Next thing I knew I was in the summer-house, but there was nobody there. Nobody at all.

*

And the next thing I did was to steal Cain and Abel's hats. I did it the next morning when I was still not entirely sober. Their hats were lying under the kitchen table where I suppose they had torn them from each other's heads, and I was seized with a bright idea – the sort you get when you're not entirely sober. They were made of scarlet crêpe paper and I imagine they'd been handed out at some pre-Christmas party. I slipped them into my pocket and if anyone asked I should say I'd thought they were rubbish and had neatly thrown them in the bin. You may be wondering what appeal these hats held for me, so I will explain that it was not for their beauty but for their utility that I desired them. I cut them up and turned them into red flowers and I told Monica that her cactus was undoubtedly going to bloom in time for the wedding. It was all part of my plot. I told her that from biblical times there had been a belief that there was no more fortunate portent on a nuptial occasion than the blossoming of a cactus. I said it was held to be so by all the people of the Book, by Muslimin and Farangi alike, and it might have been true for all I knew. Certainly a desert people might find it cheering to discover a flower when a wedding was about to take place. Monica, although she was unimaginative, was superstitious, so she swallowed this whole. I told myself she was grasping at the last straw that broke the camel's back, but that was because I still wasn't entirely sober.

I put on my new coat and went out with my

paper hats, down to the summer-house. Margaret was there already, just sitting and staring out of the window at the leaves and the birds blowing around in the cold. So I couldn't finish my flowers there.

She said, 'You look warm.'

I said I wasn't warm really. The coat helped but I felt chilled all through. I told Margaret her mother's cactus was due for a happy event and then I went to see Syl's mother.

*

We sat at the kitchen table and drank whisky and I got smoke in my eyes trying to make fiddly little flowers with a cigarette between my teeth. No easy matter, I can tell you. Syl's mother was being gloomy about Margaret. As well she might be. She was wondering if she should tell Syl about Derek's misdemeanour towards his daughter.

'Ach, *no*,' I said, 'he'd never forgive her. He'd hate her, and every time she displeased him he'd tell her she was no good. Hopeless. A deformed, unnatural and filthy thing to be used and abused as the fancy took him...' OK. That wasn't tactful either. Not to speak so to a mother of her son, but I knew it was true. I don't know how I knew, but I knew. Anyway, there wasn't going to be a wedding, so there was no point at all in telling Syl such a thing about a person who soon would be a stranger to him.

Syl's mother was rightly offended. 'Syl isn't like that,' she said. But he was. A lot of men were like that, and Syl certainly was. I *knew*. I did not, however, insist. Syl's mother went on worrying about it.

'Are you sure she doesn't remember?' she said.

I was certain. Margaret had wanted to tell me things – about Nour and love and sorrow – and I hadn't let her. I knew about love and sorrow and the subject of nasty little Nour bored me. If she'd remembered what her father had done she'd have tried to tell me about that. I wouldn't have let her because there really are some things I don't want to know. If she'd remembered she'd have been *determined* to tell me. She trusted me. Oh, oh.

Mrs Monro gave up. 'What are you making?' she asked.

'I am making wedding decorations,' I said. 'Secret ones,' and she began to cry. 'Oh, Lili,' she said.

Now you might not have thought it but I can't bear to see people cry – not children or dogs or men or old ladies. This is partly why I hasten so about the world, because I cannot stay and see people cry. I always feel I should do something about it and this is inconvenient. I particularly didn't like to see Syl's mother cry. She was supposed to be a dry old lady; a brave and funny old lady of the sort I would be myself if I lived that long. I held her hand and I said, 'There *won't* be a wedding.' I promised her. So that was that. Boats burned, bridges crossed.

She opened another bottle of whisky and I had another drink and another cigarette and then I left her and went back to the summer-house because Monica's cleaning lady had arrived. She was Mrs Monro's cleaning lady too. I sometimes felt a bit haunted by her. Margaret had gone. Back to bed probably.

*

Monica's house was now uninhabitable with Adam and Eve and the little ones. We had really nothing in common. Eve didn't like me. She couldn't see the point of me and I wasn't going to be bothered to enchant her. Why should I? It would have done neither of us any good and she'd undoubtedly have tried to tell me things I didn't want to know. So I had to go out a lot. I began to wish I was back in Iskenderiyeh. I began to miss the smell of dust and chickens and onions. I was a gypsy after all and I began to wish I was walking along a *gisr*, looking down at the river while the sun set red in a haze of dust. Yes, I knew I'd be restless there too, but I was tired of here. A small villa at Râs-et-Tin under the walls of the Khedive's summer palace would have suited me now; figs and jasmine and a mulberry tree. All gone. All gone. Oh my dear ones, the sadness of life.

I went often to Syl's house. Now I felt at peace with Syl's mother. She cared nothing for my transgressions. She trusted me. I felt safe with her. Oh yes, I was a Nazarene, but I began more and more to feel it would not have been so bad to live in the Zenana with the women – just so long as the Sultan was away a lot. Safe and quiet with the old wives and the young ones and the children. The children would have rather spoiled it, now I come to think about it. Nothing was ever perfect. Shadowed rooms with the sun fingering its way between the lattice would not be ideal if they were full of hooting children. Perhaps, after all, Margaret had chosen the best way; the convent way. I wasn't well. Not well to be thinking so. I put on my red coat and went out in the cold to see Syl's mother. The cleaning lady was there, cleaning. She grinned at me. Almost she laughed at me. I didn't mind. She was just another woman of the Zenana. There could have been few secrets in the Zenana. If she could read my thoughts I didn't care. Why should I? Slaves and eunuchs, Osmanli and Circassians, Frankish women and women of the desert – all had lived together in the harem and known each other's thoughts. There was no privacy there, and those who practised secrecy, if they were found out, suffered things I could not tell you about. You would not sleep well. I thought that secrecy was over-rated. Keeping secrets was as foolish as keeping scorpions under your hat. I wished I hadn't got any.

Syl's mother was in bed looking so old and tired. Oh my soul, the sorrows of age. I stayed with her until I had to go. I would have stayed longer but I had to go. I had to go and say goodbye to Celestine and the rest, and I thought I might go to Ely Place to confession at the church there. And then I thought I might as well wait to do that.

I said, 'I must go', and I told her not to worry, and I went.

*

I met Robert at the French pub. I hadn't known he'd be there but he was. I was so pleased to see him. Every time I saw him my heart eased a little. We had not spoken much over the last few days. Things were not well between us but still just to see him there eased my heart. He was standing by the bar, leaning on an elbow and there were people all around us.

I said, 'Hullo, my darling', and he said, 'I'm leaving you, Lili.' So he was a coward. He couldn't have told me when we were alone. He had to wait until we were surrounded by strangers. Never mind that I knew all these people. They were strangers now. They looked at me without embarrassment. They didn't love me now I'd been repudiated.

'You're a hashshâsh, Lili,' said my husband. He had lived long in my country to learn to be so cruel. 'Go and live with the Old Man of the Mountains,' he said. He was drunk.

127

I went to Celestine's but she was out, so I smoked by myself. I'd always used a little hashish. A lot of my countrymen did. It was not so harmful to the liver as drink. Robert disapproved of it in the same way that he disapproved of me 'sponging' – just because it was foreign. He would borrow money from people he didn't like, and sometimes he drank until he fell over. But that was all right.

Yes, sometimes hashish made me indiscreet and do things I would not otherwise have done, but does not drink also have this effect? Yes, it does. Robert was irrational and I was angry with him. I didn't mind being rebuked if I was really in the wrong, but he didn't know I was. He was being needlessly cruel and it wasn't fair.

I picked up the telephone and before I could speak I found I was sobbing. There were tears in the telephone. I never weep. Not usually. It was the cold of this accursed country that had weakened my resistance. 'Oh, I'm so unhappy,' I said.

There was another side to Syl. A side I haven't told you about. I always knew he had this other side, but I had never had to rely on it. I had *despised* him for it. It was a womanly side; a gentle, loving, worrying side. He would wrinkle his forehead with concern and lean over and take your hand. It was anaphrodisiac, but so comforting. He stayed with me until I stopped crying and then we talked. After a while we finished talking about me. There are limits to what can be said about me. So we talked about Syl. I found I rather liked him, I was quite fond of him. I remembered that once upon a time I had faintly loved him before I became aware of this womanly side. Now I lay against the warmth of that womanly side and felt comforted. The ironies of life. We talked for hours, and we only talked. We might have been in the Zenana.

Syl didn't love Margaret. I didn't care what anybody said. *He* said he did, but I knew he didn't. I could tell. That made it easier. Dreaming in the dark, I thought Syl was a *mustahàll*. When a man divorces you – and all he has to do is say so – he can't marry you again until you've married someone else in the meantime. He's called a *mustahàll* and everybody is happier if he is either so old or so unattractive as to render the consummation merely technical and not much fun. Oh well.

*

Oh God, life goes on. On and on. The next day was the day before the wedding. Robert had come back. It may have been because he still did love me really, but I think it was because he was English. It would not have been *comme il faut* to disappear from the house of his hostess the day before the wedding. I didn't ask him. I still had my pride. Pooh to you,

129

Robert, with your insults and your Englishness and your cowardice. Whatever else *I* was, I was brave. When nothing else is left bravery is the only virtue that counts. Ask the Mujaheddin. Even death is nothing to the brave.

Death would have been preferable to the night before the wedding with Monica's house-party. I drank so much whisky it was like committing temporary suicide. I don't remember much about it in consequence. I have tiny lightning memories of Monica being arch. She had asked Money Bags to come and stay. That was mad if you like. She'd done it to prove to Cynthia that she had an admirer. He didn't admire her at all but Cynthia didn't notice. She didn't notice anything, wrapped up as she was in Cain and Abel. Mrs Monro brought the dog and I think I may have trodden on him. I heard him yelp. I didn't care. I didn't care about anything any more. I sat by Margaret and we killed a bottle of whisky.

*

When they come to guillotine you they say: 'The time has come to be brave.' When they're about to embark on the Jehad they give you hashish. It was the day of the wedding.

I put on my wedding clothes; my crimson redingote and my silver shoes and my little Turkish hat and I went to the summer-house, and I tied the flowers I had made from the hats of Cain and Abel to the nasty cactus and I made my peace with God. In sh' Allah ... And I had given my word.

'Oh darling, oh my heart,' I said, dancing in the dining-room. 'It's out.'

'What's out?' asked Monica.

Oh God, she was difficult. The trouble I'd gone to and she asked 'What's out?' I said: 'The cactus is out', and I thought – your bloody, rotten cactus is out, and Eblis is out, and all the devils in hell, and Gehennum is empty. I said, 'Finish your breakfast and you must all come to the summer-house and see, and we will drink champagne.'

And I went back to the summer-house and Syl came as I had bidden him, for I had said to him: 'Out of the love I bear you, and for old times' sake, we must meet in the morning before the wedding, and I will give you something whereby you will never forget me', for when I smoke too much I revert to the speech form of my childhood. Oh dear God.

When he came he was carrying a dead dog. He said, 'My mother's dog died.' And I thought I had truly gone mad.

I said, 'You must bury the dog', wondering as I spoke whether the dead dog was an illusion of the jânn and Syl would know I was mad. I think he went away and then he came back and then ...

I danced for him. I danced for them all. I looked up and saw them through the window. My audience. Syl's mother saw me as she had seen me before. I had given her my word. Margaret saw me,

131

and to her too, I had given my word. The cleaning lady saw me and grinned, for she was not surprised. Robert saw me as he had never seen me before and I was avenged.

I had danced thus before in dark places. In the dark places of the world. I had thought never to do so again. I had paid my debts – both of love and hate. I was dead now. I was Lilith high on her black wings in the desert air. It was for the living to continue the dance, if dance they could. Adam and Eve and their ruined little children. And if they could not then it was nothing to me. For I had kept my word.